Jed decided he'd had enough.

If he was going to play outsider, he'd prefer to be literally outside rather than sitting at a table with these stuffy prigs. He stood. "It's been swell, Mrs. Throckmorton, but I've got a full day tomorrow."

Augustina followed and cornered him in the vestibule. "I'll walk you back to the carriage house," she said.

"You confuse me," Jed confessed.

How marvelous, Augustina almost blurted. She'd always been a mouse, yet Jed was actually noticing her.

She snatched off her glasses.

But what next? What would her sister do at a moment like this? "I'm sorry you missed dessert," she whispered.

"Yeah, well, I sort of got the feeling that I'd said something wrong."

She didn't want to explain about their neighbor Vanessa Van Pelt and her penchant for sleeping with her gardeners, not when a similar notion had seized Augustina's own mind. Strangely, even that delighted her. Who in all of Sheepshead Bay would believe that Gussy Gutless actually had something in common with Vanessa Van Vixen?

"Well," she said, "I'd like to make it up to you."

Jed cocked one brow. "Did you have something in mind?"

Did she ever. *Do it,* she thought. *Do it.* She wasn't very good at this type of thing, but before she could chicken out, she said, "Sweets for the sweet," and pounced on him.

Dear Reader,

Our Let's Celebrate! promotion is coming to an end this month, so take advantage of your last chance to enter our sweepstakes. A fabulous collection of romantic comedy videos is the prize.

Carrie Alexander, a RITA nominee, continues the adventures of the peculiar but fascinating Fairchild family from *The Madcap Heiress* with Augustina Fairchild's story. *The Amorous Heiress* is a truly delightful romp.

Longtime and incredibly successful romance author Kristine Rolofson joins our Matchmaking Mothers (from Hell) lineup with *Pillow Talk*. As a mother of six who has also published over twenty books, Kristine is obviously a woman who is able to balance a busy career and family life very well. (Perhaps with a lot of love and laughter?) She certainly handled the matchmaking mother concept with ease. We can't help but wonder if her own children are getting a little nervous?

Wishing you another month filled with much love and laughter,

Malle Vallik

Malle Vallik
Associate Senior Editor

THE AMOROUS HEIRESS
Carrie Alexander

Harlequin Books

TORONTO • NEW YORK • LONDON
AMSTERDAM • PARIS • SYDNEY • HAMBURG
STOCKHOLM • ATHENS • TOKYO • MILAN
MADRID • WARSAW • BUDAPEST • AUCKLAND

ISBN 0-373-44028-6

THE AMOROUS HEIRESS

A funny thing happened...

Imagination and inspiration are tools of the trade for a writer. That's why I love movies. Where else do you find villas and vineyards, costume balls, beach umbrellas, sleeping compartments, gondolas, cigarette holders and striped garden tents abounding? How often in real life do you hobnob with women in Dior and diamonds and men in spiffy white dinner jackets? When was the last time you sunbathed on the French Riviera or checked in to an Italian castle filled with wisteria and sunshine? Just thinking about those things enables me to look outside at the waist-high snow and smile.

This particular book was inspired by touches of the truth (I really do know a soap-eating dog!), the fortuitous (I took the title *The Amorous Heiress* from a movie synopsis in the TV listings) and of course, the cinematic. (Look for the *Sense and Sensibility* kiss scene—it's my favorite.)

Here's wishing you your own moments of romantic inspiration, whether they come from a movie, a book...or the Cary Grant of your dreams. And here's to another year of sparkling romantic comedies from LOVE & LAUGHTER!

—Carrie Alexander

Books by Carrie Alexander

LOVE & LAUGHTER
8—THE MADCAP HEIRESS

HARLEQUIN TEMPTATION
536—FANCY-FREE
590—ALL SHOOK UP

Don't miss any of our special offers. Write to us at the following address for information on our newest releases.

Harlequin Reader Service
U.S.: 3010 Walden Ave., P.O. Box 1325, Buffalo, NY 14269
Canadian: P.O. Box 609, Fort Erie, Ont. L2A 5X3

1

The Mouse and the Matriarch

AUGUSTINA FAIRCHILD threw open the chintz curtains with a theatrical flourish and stepped up to the center of the window. The old saying was trite but true: this was the first day of the rest of her life.

And from now on she was not only going to direct the show, she was going to play the starring role.

She raised the window and took a deep breath. The morning was sunny and clear. Even though she couldn't see the ocean from her second-floor bedroom at the front of Throckmorton Cottage, she could hear the crash of the surf and smell its salty tang mixed with the scents of sweet lavender from the garden and of the pungent piney wood beyond.

Her view was as familiar as ever—dark treetops, the long green lawn bordered by a terrace wall, straight gravel paths that converged at a small fountain, then the sheared mounds of boxwood and, closest to the house, the herbaceous border's skeins of color, glistening with dew. It was only her inner viewpoint that had changed.

"You go, girl," she said out loud, trying to bolster herself for the challenge ahead. The present-day vernacular didn't suit either Augustina or the Gilded Age sensibilities of Throckmorton Cottage, but there you were. It was time for her to stop changing to suit the family estate and its inhabitants. Well past time.

She rested her hands on the sun-warmed sill. She was almost twenty-five years old and she was as useless as her grandmother's Victorian gimcracks and bibelots. In other words, strictly decorative, cluttering things up and collecting more dust with each passing day.

Her major accomplishments up to now had been overseeing the gardens—with the aid of a part-time gardener, so that hardly counted—and finally finishing the needlepoint rug she'd worked on for one year, two months and fifteen days. Not a lot to be proud of when she considered that one of her classmates from Miss Fibbing-White's had already married and gestated and launched a sideline career designing amusing little handbags that had been featured in *Vogue*. Another was in Brazil protecting rain forests. Augustina—Gussy to them—had received postcards. Even the awful Phoebe Beecham had been photographed with Duchess Fergie for the tabloids, whereas Gussy's greatest social triumph up to now had been her appointment as head of the garden club's regatta refreshment table.

She looked at the oval, flower-patterned rug carelessly tossed over the back of a skirted slipper chair. Yesterday had been stormy; she'd been stuck inside all afternoon with Grandmother Throckmorton. Sitting in the library before the fire, Gussy had stitched the last stitch and knotted the last knot, then knelt to lay the completed piece across the faded baize carpet. Grandmother had set aside her own needlepoint project and reached down to smooth a wrinkle from the rug. "There you go, Augustina," she'd said, so pleasantly smug and snug that in contrast Augustina had felt positively itchy with undefined yearnings. "Wasn't all that handwork worth the effort? Doesn't producing something so pretty and practical give you an immense sense of accomplishment?''

Suddenly, irrationally, she had wanted to explode. She'd wanted to stand up and shout "No!" at the top of her lungs, though of course she'd contained herself. She always did. The sheer inertia of playing the obedient granddaughter had her in its grip, and besides, Grandmother Throckmorton considered shouting shockingly rude. Gussy had tamped down her rebellion, rolled up the rug and gone meekly to bed.

She hadn't slept. She'd flopped from stomach to spine and squiggled from side to side until 2:00 a.m., when she'd opened her eyes and made up her mind, once and for all, that she was going to take charge of her life. For real. She didn't want to wake up thirty years from now and discover herself to be a carbon copy of Grandmother Throckmorton—rigid, stern and so comfortably settled that her life held absolutely no excitement, little turbulence or complication and certainly no surprise.

Starting first thing in the morning, Augustina Isobel Throckmorton Fairchild would change her life.

Settling on the exact details of how she should go about doing so hadn't occurred to her until the alarm clock awakened her at seven o'clock on the dot, as it had every morning for the past four years. Then she remembered her doubts, and an inconvenient tidbit she'd learned at a boarding-school science class. One of the properties of inertia—in this case Gussy's—was that she would continue to carry out her uniform motions unless acted upon by an outside force. She wasn't sure that the cycle could be broken by strength from within, especially when her own force of will had up to now mustered barely enough strength to refuse oatmeal at breakfast.

Augustina knew that change would take a certain courage of conviction. Having never found the need to develop courage, or, for that matter, conviction, she certainly didn't know how to acquire it at this late date. Growing up, she'd found it easiest to behave in an agreeable and placable manner and be rewarded by her grandparents for being a "good girl." She'd known from the cradle that she wasn't glamorous and flamboyant like April, her older sister. Nor was she sophisticated and adventurous like her globetrotting parents.

She was Gussy, plain old Gussy, quiet and solid as a rock, often overlooked. Which rocks usually were...until someone tripped over them.

Well, she'd stumbled and fallen flat on her face last night and hadn't liked it at all. So the alternative was clear. She must change her life. She must find a way to defy her grandmother's expectations.

Not to mention her great-grandfather's.

At the thought of Great-grandfather two doors away, Gussy conscientiously turned back to close the window before going down to breakfast. Elias Quincy Throckmorton was ninety-four, bedridden, hard of hearing, riddled with cataracts and gout, but he could sense within minutes if there was a window open anywhere on the second floor. One could say he was a draft savant.

But he was also the undeniable head of the household. Even Grandmother deferred to him, and Gussy...Gussy positively quaked in his presence.

Sliding the window shut, she glimpsed a figure in white crossing the terraced lawn from the direction of the parking court. Sunshine reflected off blond hair. *Andrews Lowell,* she thought, not without a touch of comfortable condescension.

Andrews was Grandmother's chosen suitor for Augustina's fair hand. He was almost as reliable and rocklike as

Gussy herself, and though having Andrews to count on was convenient, it was also hopelessly predictable. Fifty-odd years ago, Marian May Andrews had married E. Q. Throckmorton, Jr., and eventually become known— at least to Gussy and her sister—as Grandmother-with-a-capital-*G*. So if Augustina Fairchild were to complete the circle by marrying Andrews Lowell, fifty years from now Gussy would become...

She shuddered delicately. It was too gruesome a future to contemplate.

As she double-checked the window, since Great-grandfather would know if even a cubic inch of fresh air made its way inside, Gussy's gaze was again drawn by a movement on the graveled path. Another male figure was approaching the house, but this one was unknown to her.

She blinked. Absolutely unknown. Thrillingly so.

The stranger, and there weren't many of them in tiny Sheepshead Bay, Maine, except during tourist season, was reminiscent of the type of male that the teenaged Gussy and April had been warned about by both Grandmother and the headmistress at Miss Fibbing-White's. Naturally, that meant April had carried on a forbidden flirtation with every stable boy and black-leather-jacketed townie who sneaked past their chaperons. For her part, Gussy had only admired the type from afar...and developed the kind of inappropriate fantasy life even Grandmother Throckmorton couldn't control.

Not that this man looked disreputable, exactly. He just didn't look like anyone Gussy had ever made the acquaintance of. He was too rugged. Too rangy. Too...male.

Practically a foreign species, in Gussy's experience of overly Waspish trust-fund milksops like Andrews Lowell.

Which was probably why her nose was squashed against the windowpane. She forced herself to step back, then leaned closer again, squinting to make out the details. "Hold on, hold on," she muttered to the stranger, darting to her nightstand to retrieve her glasses. She slipped on the gold wire frames and rushed back to the window.

Ah, yes—he was still there. In fact, he was kneeling beside one of the peonies that flanked the broad front steps, rooting about in the mulch. How strange. Perhaps he'd dropped something. She hoped not a wedding ring.

Gussy pressed her cheek to the window, trying to get a better angle for a closer look. *Of his buns,* she thought, suppressing a surprised giggle as his head and shoulders disappeared beneath the bushy peony. Gracious, it was turning out that the new Augustina Fairchild was the teensiest bit naughty.

"Still, he does have nice ones," she whispered, admiring the body-hugging fit of his jeans even though that wasn't exactly the kind of stimulation she'd decided her life was lacking. But now that she thought about it...it was.

The man stood and climbed the steps, dusting off his hands before he put them in his back pockets and surveyed the front terrace garden and the wood beyond. A nature lover, Gussy decided with a sigh. They'd have something in common.

He had dark brown hair, cut short, and wide shoulders beneath an olive green camp shirt with the sleeves rolled up almost to his biceps. Gussy couldn't tell for sure even with her glasses on, but she had a premonition that his muscular arms bore at least one tattoo. Grandmother Throckmorton thought tattoos were terribly lowbrow. Gussy was secretly of another opinion.

She sighed. Even at this distance, the mysterious stranger seemed so vigorously sexy that she couldn't help but surrender to her vivid imagination and picture him reclining naked in her canopy bed. His skin would look very brown in contrast to her pristine white sheets, the dark hair on his chest and arms crisp against the smooth cotton, the tattoos decorating his sculpted muscles so very masculine among her ruffled pillows. His hands would be callused and roughened but gentle, very gentle, as he lifted the crocheted hem of the sheet and gestured for her to join him....

She shook her head. Naughty? Why, the new Augustina Fairchild was positively wicked!

When she looked again, the as-yet-faceless stranger had disappeared. Something inside her shivered. He was knocking at the front door, asking for her. Or so she hoped, and not without reason.

Ever since Grandmother had decided that Gussy was getting a bit long in the tooth for a readily marriageable young lady and had put out the word among her cronies, various single males—family friends mainly, except for the occasional visiting cousin from Newport or Westchester—had begun presenting themselves at Throckmorton Cottage for Gussy's approval. While she hadn't found any of the prospects all that exciting, she'd compliantly accepted their invitations for picnics and sailing, for golfing at the country club. She'd gone on more dates in the past four weeks than she had in the previous four years. Which still wasn't all that many compared to April's Deb-of-the-Year whirl, but there you were.

Resisting the urge to pinch herself, Gussy went to peer inside her closet. The itchy feeling was back, crawling under the top layer of her skin. She told herself that chances were very remote that the stranger on the doorstep was yet another version of the out-of-town cousin, simply an intriguing little bend in the family tree of one of Sheepshead Bay's founding families. And Grandmother Throckmorton wouldn't approve even if he was, but, then, Gussy had decided to take charge of her own life, hadn't she?

And although she might not be a raving beauty, there was no reason to meet him wearing an ancient Camp Skowhegan sweatshirt and frayed L.L. Bean shorts. A flattering sundress with a long full skirt would do much better. Grandmother would approve only if she neglected to notice the halter top, which left Gussy's back essentially bare. That wasn't likely, so Gussy tied a lightweight watermelon-colored sweater around her shoulders. The new Gussy could compromise as long as she didn't knuckle under.

She brushed her long straight hair and slipped on one of her customary headbands without considering otherwise. Mascara, for once? Yes. And a smudge of smoky blue eyeliner at the corner of each eye was warranted as well.

Gussy smiled at herself in the mirror of her dressing table. Well, she wasn't gorgeous, but anticipating an encounter with the mystery man downstairs had goosed her pulse enough to produce two spots of rosy color in her cheeks and a sparkle in her eyes. Without her glasses— she tossed them down—she was presentable.

In the hallway, Gussy met Rozalinda, Elias Throckmorton's soft-spoken, round-as-a-beachball Jamaican night nurse, and Schwarthoff, the starchy, broad-beamed German day nurse, as they changed shifts. Nurse Schwarthoff nodded briskly without pause and continued down the hall with the breakfast tray, her orthopedic shoes soundless on the Oriental runner. Rozalinda rolled her eyes, her big, pink-gummed smile lighting up her ebony face. Schwarthoff knocked once for form before entering the invalid patriarch's sanctum. The heavy mahogany door thunked shut behind her.

"How's Great-grandfather?" Gussy whispered. "Should I go in to say good morning?" She was supposed to, most days, but it wasn't something she looked forward to.

"Schwarthoff will have one of her conniptions if you interrupt breakfast while the oatmeal is hot," Rozalinda said. "You can try later, but somet'ing tell me Elias sleep most of the day." She nudged Gussy and pointed into her large woven carryall. An oversize deck of cards and a score pad attested to the night's activities. Elias's sole remaining pleasure was two-handed, penny-a-point canasta.

"Roz!" Gussy said, pretending censure. Then she smiled. "How much did you take him for?"

Rozalinda rattled the bulge of coins in the pocket of her white polyester uniform. "Enough to pay the fee on another of my daughter's college applications." Her mellifluous laugh burbled like a waterfall in the vast space of the two-story front hall as they made their way down the staircase.

Gussy wished she could be as easy in her great-grandfather's company. Rozalinda had counseled Gussy not to take any of his guff, but whenever Great-grandfather shouted thunderously and pounded the floor with his cane she quavered like the mouse that she was.

The mouse that you were, she reminded herself. Still, she was glad to have escaped his inspection for the day. It would be better to test out her new attitude on someone less formidable.

Not Grandmother, not yet, but maybe someone like... Thwaite.

After Rozalinda had departed by the side door nearest the parking court, Gussy tiptoed across the polished marquetry floor of the front hall and started edging open the various doors leading off it. The library was dim and unoccupied, smelling faintly of wood smoke from last evening's fire. The hearth was scraped clean, with new apple-wood logs set in the andirons, so Thwaite had already been there. Next door was the formal drawing room, empty as usual. Gold-flecked dust motes danced in the strong sunshine flooding the tall windows, making the ancient watered silk drapes look particularly shabby. The Throckmortons preferred tradition to change; even when new drapes were finally made, it would be from an antique fabric and in the same style that the very first Throckmorton had chosen.

Gussy crossed the drawing room, inched open one of the French doors of the solarium and stuck her head inside. She gaped at the occupants, gasped audibly and, before they could react, slammed the door so hard its wavy glass panes rattled.

"Miss Augustina?"

Gussy whirled around. Darn it. Thwaite had crept up behind her on his sneaky, quiet-as-cat's-paws feet. Grandmother labeled Thwaite's stealth discretion; Gussy thought of it as just plain creepy.

She told herself that she was no longer the seven-year-old whom Thwaite had once caught red-handed in the gazebo, spying on April playing doctor with Vito Carlucci, the chauffeur's son. Drawing a deep breath, keeping hold of the door latch behind her back, she confronted him. "Thwaite, exactly whom have you put in the solarium?"

The butler pursed his lips, making his wrinkled turtle face look like a lemon with all the juice sucked out. "Your gentlemen callers, Miss Augustina."

Accustomed as she was to living in Thwaite's coastal-Maine version of *The Glass Menagerie,* Gussy said only, "But there are three of them." Her heart was still pounding like a kettledrum from that discovery, and she was certain it wasn't because of the presence of Andrews Lowell and Billy Tuttle.

Thwaite nodded. "As you say, Miss Augustina."

"Well, I recognize Billy and Andrews...but who's the third?"

"The gentleman—" Thwaite's paper-thin nostrils fluttered slightly "—gave his name as Kelley, I believe. I put him in with the others, miss."

Gussy nipped her bottom lip with her teeth. There were no Kelleys in Sheepshead Bay, not among the Throckmorton's admittedly limited circle. "And when was I to be informed of his...their arrival?"

"In due time, Miss Augustina. Your grandmother is waiting on the terrace." Thwaite slipped a silver pocket watch from his waistcoat, flicked the cover up and checked the time. "You're already eight minutes late for breakfast." He closed the watch with a snap and tucked it away again, the links of its fob jingling softly.

Gussy could on occasion avoid Great-grandfather, but breakfast with Grandmother was without exception de rigueur. Even for the new Gussy.

Her gentlemen callers would have to wait. Thinking that perhaps she'd fallen into an odd game of Mystery Date instead of a Tennessee Williams play, Gussy nodded coolly to the butler and made her way to the dining room at the back of the house. Another pair of French doors was standing open to a pink granite terrace overlooking the ocean. The water was a cheery blue today, a welcome change after three days of rain and fog. The surf battered the steep cliffs, breaking into geysers of spume that glittered in the sunshine.

Marian May Andrews Throckmorton sat in the shade of the patio table's umbrella, serenely drinking coffee while she waited for her granddaughter. She was a handsome woman, deceptively slender for someone with her strength of character and constitution, traits that were also reflected in a regal bearing that remained unbowed after seventy-one years. Her dress was a stylish but subdued designer original.

Gussy hesitated in the doorway, nibbling on her lower lip, then briskly stepped outside when Thwaite arrived to hover at her elbow. "G'morning, Grandmother," she said, and kissed the older woman's tilted cheek, sniffing talc, lavender water and antiseptic mouthwash.

"Good morning, Augustina. Mind your mumbling."

"Pardon me, ma'am," Gussy said automatically. Thwaite pulled out her chair. She started to sit and he scooted the chair beneath her until she was wedged in tight against the table, just as locked in place as if she'd never made the resolution to take charge of her life. The butler slipped her napkin from its ring, snapped out the accordion pleats and dropped it into her lap.

"That will be all, thank you, Thwaite," Marian said, dismissing him in the midst of lifting the domed lids of the serving dishes to reveal warm muffins, buttery yellow scrambled eggs and thick pottery bowls of oatmeal. Thwaite stayed long enough to position one of the bowls at Gussy's place setting, then turned on his heel and vanished into the house, missing the cutting look Gussy knifed at his retreating back.

Stubbornly she set aside the oatmeal. The Victorian Throckmortons had been sticklers about prescribing oatmeal and cod liver oil to the younger generations, which explained a lot about Great-grandfather's sour personality. While Gussy's doses of cod liver oil had ended at age eighteen, the oatmeal was still a constant. She'd learned to dread its appearance at the table.

Marian looked askance, but for once did not utter a word

of protest—possibly because her mouth was all gummed up with a spoonful of oatmeal. Gussy poured a glass of juice from the sterling-silver pitcher. Prune this morning, yuck. It was difficult living with a woman whose comportment was so rigid she always did what was best for her health or most suited to her station in life. Beside Grandmother, Augustina felt her own conduct was middling at best, and middling was not good enough for a Throckmorton-Fairchild. Which explained a lot about Gussy's personality, since middling was the story of her life.

"I think I'll have just a blueberry muffin," she announced.

Marian dished out the eggs anyway, passing a plate to her granddaughter.

"I'm already running late," Gussy persisted. And there was a very interesting gentleman caller waiting for her in the solarium…although she wasn't going to tell her grandmother that.

Not to be rushed, Marian scanned the serving dishes and added a sausage to Gussy's plate. "It will do the boys good to wait for you."

Thwaite was a tattletale, Gussy thought with disgust. Then her eyebrows went up. Did Grandmother already know about…? She couldn't. Gussy was certain that not even her grandmother would call the definitively manly stranger named Kelley a boy.

"It's best for a young lady not to appear too eager."

Gussy bowed her head. "Yes, ma'am." If April had been there, she'd've been muffling giggles in her napkin and plotting a rendezvous with the tempting stranger. It would take place right under Grandmother's nose and probably employ a maid's apron, a feather duster and a chauffeur's uniform. Gussy, however, listened without protest and silently marshaled her forces. She was planning to choose her battles more judiciously.

The scalloped edge of the striped umbrella flapped in the breeze. Marian waved her napkin at a wayward honeybee. "How is Andrews's courtship progressing?" she asked.

At the word *courtship,* Gussy choked on a piece of the crumbled muffin. Her grandmother was sincerely deluded if she believed that Gussy would become engaged to Andrews. At least not so soon. Not before she tried someone—some*thing*—else.

"We don't have an understanding, if that's what you mean, Grandmother." Gussy cleared her throat. "Anyway, I think I might go sailing with…"

Since Grandmother's serene countenance did not waver at the pause, Gussy decided it was safe to presume that the older woman didn't know about the maybe-tattooed hunk in the solarium. If she had, she'd have been issuing orders for her granddaughter to keep her distance.

"…Billy Tuttle," Gussy finished, crossing her fingers under cover of the tablecloth.

"Splendid," Marian approved. "We can't have Andrews being too sure of you."

Just what Gussy needed—a dinosaur like Grandmother Throckmorton giving her dating tips. Silently she finished her blueberry muffin and began rearranging what was left of the scrambled eggs to hide the uneaten sausage. Grandmother's ideas on the subject of dating were strictly old-fashioned. She even thought that Gussy was still a virgin, which was probably Gussy's fault, since she hadn't dared to inform her grandmother otherwise. Of course, she wouldn't be in the predicament of pretending she was one if she'd had the gumption to break free years ago, the way her sister had. Gussy sighed softly. She had somehow always managed to just miss the moment of escape.

Marian looked at her granddaughter's plate. "Mind your manners, Augustina. You mustn't toy with your food."

"Pardon me, ma'am." Gussy set aside her utensils, then said, most tentatively, "Grandmother..."

"Speak up, child. Don't dawdle."

"Grandmother, I've decided to..." Gussy's throat clenched. *Spit it out,* she thought. *Tell her you've decided to take charge of your own life from here on out. Do it. Do it. Now or never.*

Then again, there *were* the laws of inertia, she remembered, starting to waffle. Okay, she was a mouse, still a mouse, *always* a mouse, but this would be so much easier on her if the pattern of her inertia was broken by an outside force.

An outside force like...marriage.

The notion had popped into Gussy's head out of nowhere; her eyes widened at its possibilities, then narrowed at its impossibilities. Marriage? What was she thinking? Getting married was exactly what Grandmother wanted her to do!

But that was the beauty of it, Gussy realized in the next moment. To all outward appearances, she'd be conforming, when in reality marriage would be the perfect vehicle for her to declare her freedom.

Grandmother Throckmorton and the rest of the grand dames of Sheepshead Bay revered marriage as a sacred trust. A married woman was instantly, almost without exception, accorded their respect. And once granted, only the worst of transgressions—made publicly or, worse, scandalized in print—could cause a woman to lose that standing. Maybe not even then. Look at Mrs. Ann Owen Gilmore, perpetually three sheets to the wind at every yacht-club function; Mrs. Catherine Chalk, belle of the Episcopal Sisterhood's charity ball even though she was suspected of embezzling from their quilting fund; and Mrs. Vanessa Van Pelt, who carried on flaming affairs with every gardener she hired, but was nonetheless still the president of the Junior League.

Why, a certificate of marriage was practically a license to run wild!

Going the wedded-bliss route had worked for Gussy's sister. Already having the courage that Gussy lacked, April's first step to freedom had been enrolling at a California university instead of the traditional Throckmorton choice, Vassar. Then, after four years of relative freedom and before the grandparents could begin issuing ultimatums, April had accepted the best of her various marriage proposals and returned triumphant to Maine with both a degree and a fiancé. Because the fiancé was from a family nearly as rich and connected as the Throckmortons, Great-grandfather had bestowed his grudging approval. After a lavish society wedding, April had departed in a blaze of glory to live her own life on her own terms.

Gussy, a junior at Vassar at the time, had remained firmly under her grandparents' thumbs. Where she'd stayed to this day.

But no longer, Gussy confirmed silently.

If marriage was the easiest way to squirm out from under, then so be it.

She squared her shoulders. The fact that there was a dreamboat of a gentleman caller awaiting her approval in the solarium had very little to do with her decision. The mysterious Mr. Kelley's arrival was simply fortuitous happenstance.

"Augustina," Marian finally snapped, "please be so

kind as to finish your sentences. Honestly, but you're woolgathering this morning.''

Resisting the impulse to blurt out another ''Pardon me, ma'am,'' as she'd been taught to always do, Gussy instead looked straight into her grandmother's clear hazel eyes, which widened slightly as Marian patted her lips with a napkin, then tilted her chin at a haughty, lady-of-the-manor angle. Without averting her gaze from her granddaughter's, Marian smoothed her palms over the princess roll of dove gray locks haloing her face; as usual, there was not a hair out of place.

The silence between them lengthened. Gussy's muscles tensed as she fought not to avert her stare.

Then it happened.

Grandmother Throckmorton blinked. She looked away. She even fiddled with her napkin, waving it about distractedly.

Whether it was silly or not, Gussy was elated. She'd gripped the arms of the chair until her knuckles were white, but for once in her life she hadn't given in. She'd won a contest of wills. So what if it had been only a minor skirmish?

''Grandmother,'' Gussy said firmly, which was much easier to do when she knew she was about to say what the older woman wanted to hear, ''I've decided that you're right. It *is* time for me to select a husband. In fact, I'm going to see to it at once.'' She stood and shoved her chair back, scraping it across the stones with a screech. Naturally, Grandmother would assume she was speaking of dear, stuffy old Andrews. There would be another clash if things worked out in a different direction, but that tussle could be put off for another day.

Marian nodded with satisfaction and picked up her coffee cup. "I was certain you'd see the wisdom of my advice, Augustina."

Suddenly lighthearted with munificence, Gussy leaned down to kiss the older woman's cheek, hugging her lightly around the shoulders for good measure. "You are so wise, Grandmother," she murmured, and twirled around to go back into the house, her skirt flaring out.

Marian's face had softened at the unexpected affection, but then stiffened with reproach when Gussy whipped off her sweater as she stepped inside, revealing her bare back. Marian tensed, remonstrations on her lips. A second later she relaxed back in her chair and reached again for the coffee. It wouldn't hurt Augustina to appear immodest just this once. Perhaps the Lowell boy would be inspired enough to propose now that Augustina was prepared to comply. At times like these, a good, measured, unblinking stare could work wonders on a reluctant bride, even when it was interrupted by a persistent honeybee.

The morning had been unexpectedly prosperous; Marian rewarded herself by adding an extra dollop of cream to her coffee.

Although she prided herself on her active social life and the fact that she looked not a day over sixty, Marian May Andrews Throckmorton was more than ready to settle down to being a great-grandmother.

She liked the idea of being called a matriarch.

2

Of Mice and Men

GUSSY WASN'T THINKING about providing her grandmother with great-grandchildren when she paused outside the lace-curtained glass doors to the solarium. She was thinking of men.

She'd known Andrews since they were baptized two weeks apart. They'd attended school together, back when Gussy's parents had mostly stayed put in their Manhattan co-op and used Throckmorton Cottage as their summer home. When Philip Fairchild's itch for adventure had grown too strong to ignore, he'd quit his executive job in advertising to travel the globe. Nathalie, Gussy's mother, had decided that she must go along to take photographs and fax her husband's I-Skied-the-Matterhorn articles to upscale travel magazines. Gussy and April had been shipped off to Miss Fibbing-White's, a boarding school in rural England, around the same time that Andrews Lowell was enrolling in Groton. Still, Gussy had seen enough of Andrews during the long summers of sailing and tennis in Sheepshead Bay that her feelings for him might have remained strictly sisterly if he hadn't been the first boy who kissed her. And the first boy who…

"Let's not travel that train of thought," Gussy whispered aloud, then whirled around, coughing and clearing her throat in case Thwaite had sneaked up behind her and was trying to eavesdrop.

Andrews opened the French doors. "Gussy—there you are! What happened? We've all been waiting for you to reappear."

Gussy peeped into the solarium. Billy Tuttle stood craning his neck a few paces behind Andrews, his hands stuffed in the pockets of his windbreaker. Billy was an off-and-on sales rep, mostly off during the summer so the prime sporting months weren't all bollixed up with something as dull as work. He fancied himself a ladies' man, and often imported young models from New York for the weekend to prove it. He probably wouldn't have been interested in Gussy if his own grandmother hadn't threatened him with nonpayment of his yacht-club bar bill unless he started dating someone respectable like the Fairchild girl.

Billy tapped the toe of his deck shoe in irritation. "The wind is going wasting. Do you want to sail with me or not, Gussy?"

"I've reserved a court," Andrews said, indicating his tennis whites. "We can have lunch at Felicity's after—"

"You can play tennis anytime," Billy interrupted. "This is sailing weather."

"Umm…" Gussy said vaguely as she walked into the glassed-in solarium. A jungle of hanging plants and potted palms were sprinkled among clusters of white wicker furniture upholstered with floral-and-lattice-patterned cushions. The harsh sunlight was dizzying.

Gussy squinted. Her very own mystery date had apparently given up and gone home. Disappointed, she jerked several of the brittle canvas shades down over the windows, reducing the glare to a mellow glow, and then she saw him. Or his legs, anyway.

He was sitting in the covered wicker chaise, the depth

of its hood concealing his upper half. His very attractive lower half—his legs were *long*—sported tight, faded jeans gone out at the knees and...brown leather work boots. *Huh?*

"H-hello?" Gussy quavered. She sounded like a pusillanimous pipsqueak. Like a pusillani*mouse*. Gathering her courage, telling herself that this was the first day of her new life, she strode toward the chaise, holding her chin up and her hand out. "Hello. So nice to meet you." Her voice was brisk but friendly. "Sorry to have kept you waiting, Mr....?"

The third of Gussy's gentlemen callers rose to his feet. "Kelley," he said. "Jed Kelley."

If Gussy had been wearing shoes less practical than beige leather oxfords, she'd have fallen off the heels. She did have to take a wobbling step backward, putting out her hands for balance.

Jed Kelley was her secret fantasy man come to life.

His face was handsome, but also sort of battered looking in a way that turned Gussy's soft heart to mush. His jaw was hard and square; his nose had been broken at least two times. The dark brown hair she'd already noticed was shaved so short it was almost military, all the better to reveal the precise elegance of his hairline as it followed the contours of his temples and high forehead. A narrow scar curved from his left temple to his eyelid and disappeared up into his brow, as if a white thread had drifted into his plane of vision and he'd blinked it away. His lashes were longer than his hair. And his eyes were blue— the most shocking electric blue.

Maybe that was why Gussy felt jolted to the core.

"You're not the woman I expected," he said in a gravelly voice, with a flat inflection.

Put on though it was, her confidence quailed. Was he

disappointed in her already? If that was the case, she'd just set a new land-speed record.

"I'm afraid I am." Her voice was hoarse. "I'm Augustina Throckmorton Fairchild."

The name sparked recognition in his blue eyes. "I see. Well, then…" He squared his shoulders and saluted. "Jed Kelley, reporting for duty as requested."

Gussy licked her lips and swallowed. She couldn't imagine what friend of Grandmother's had thought it appropriate to present her with Jed Kelley as a prospective groom. Perhaps some doting old aunt who hadn't seen her nephew since he was in short pants had sent him over to give Marian Throckmorton's spinster granddaughter a break.

But…"reporting for duty"? Gussy didn't like the sound of that. She wasn't desperate enough to be anyone's *duty*.

Her eyebrows arched and she looked at him the same way Grandmother eyed a serving maid who'd dropped the soup ladle on the floor. "May I ask who, uh…recommended you?"

"You don't know?" Jed's eyes narrowed. "Vanessa Van Pelt, for one."

Vanessa Van Pelt? Now Gussy was thoroughly confused. Vanessa Van Pelt would never willingly surrender a man who looked like Jed Kelley; she'd clutch him in her hot greedy hands and keep him all to herself. Unless he was a close relative, perhaps?

"And Mrs. Throckmorton, I guess you could say," Jed continued.

A tiny mew escaped Gussy's mouth. "You…you…you know Grandmother?"

"I interviewed with her last week."

"You're kidding," Gussy breathed with disbelief.

"And now that I recall, she did say something about you taking over from here on out."

Gussy shuffled away from Jed until the back of her knees hit the edge of a wicker rocker. She collapsed into it, setting it swaying back and forth with a rapid squeak-squeak-squeak.

Abruptly, as if someone had cut the strings of three marionettes, the gentlemen callers sat as one in whichever chair was closest at hand. Silence descended on the solarium, broken only by the slowing pace of the wicker rocker. Squeak…squeak…squeak. A sound rather suited to a mouse like herself, Gussy thought morosely.

There was something amiss. No more than Vanessa Van Pelt would Grandmother hand over a man like Jed on a silver platter. Not in a million years, and darn it all to heck, because boy oh boy, did Gussy want him!

She wanted him so much, at so little notice, that she positively shocked herself.

He was watching her, his finely drawn brows lifted, waiting for her to speak. So were Andrews and Billy, Andrews relatively complacent, Billy impatient. Them she could handle.

Gussy found her voice. "I'm sorry, but I can't go out with either of you today. Thank you anyway, Andrews." She rose, nodding at each of them in turn. "Billy."

"Tomorrow?" Andrews asked, his gaze twitching in the direction of Jed Kelley.

Billy shouldered Andrews aside. "The yacht club is having a dance next—"

"I don't know…I can't…okay, call me," Gussy said, just to get rid of them. She shepherded them toward the door, wondering why they'd chosen the absolute worst moment to turn into devoted swains. Thwaite, predictably, was hovering on the other side of the French doors.

"Please see these gentlemen to the front door, Thwaite," Gussy said, having to practically shove Andrews out of the solarium.

"See you soon, Gussy?" he called over his shoulder.

"I'm sure," she sighed, and shut the doors with a resolute click, hesitating there with her nose an inch away from the glass panes and her hands glued to the warm brass latch because she'd sensed that Jed's neon eyes were burning holes between her shoulder blades.

Her skin felt positively twitchy—all over. *A mouse no longer,* she vowed, and slowly turned to face Jed. "Mr. Kelley…"

He stood. "I've come at a bad time."

A smile fluttered across Gussy's lips. "On the contrary." She inched closer, swaying slightly because everything seemed so off-kilter, but swaying in a way Jed might interpret as seductive if she was lucky. "You've timed your arrival perfectly."

"And your boyfriends?"

She waved her hand. "Just two of a dozen." Technically true, now that she was being auctioned off to Sheepshead Bay's elite. "They're of no particular consequence." Not anymore.

His eyes glinted. "So that's how it is."

She smiled determinedly. "Yes, that's how it is."

"You're a very popular lady."

"Not afraid of a little competition, are you?" She inched closer, intrinsically aware of the masculine breadth and heat of Jed's body. He was strong and fit in a way that Andrews and Billy were not—fit from actual strenuous work, if the boots were a necessity and not an affectation. Taking into account the quiescent strength in his tanned arms and long, muscled legs, Gussy didn't think they were.

"Competition?" he asked in puzzlement. "Wait a minute, there. I thought the position was mine."

"You didn't think Grandmother was the final arbiter of the decision, did you?" Gussy shook her head, smiling coyly. "I'm not entirely without a say in this, you know."

"But she—"

"And I say that a trial period is in order." Emboldened with her momentum, Gussy didn't pause to think sensibly. If Jed Kelley had already, miraculously, passed Grandmother's muster, then there was nothing to slow them down. They could be married before the summer was out. Gussy would be free, with the added bonus of a husband it wouldn't be all that difficult to learn to love.

"Mrs. Throckmorton didn't say anything about a trial period."

"It makes sense." Gritting her teeth, Gussy dared herself to reach out for his hand.

"I suppose…"

And just like that, she was holding Jed's hand. She, Miss Gussy Gutless Fairchild, was holding Jed Kelley's hand.

"…I might agree," he finished awkwardly, looking down at their linked hands, his brown and callused, hers a smooth cream. "After all, you don't really know me. You don't know what kind of work I can do."

A funny way to put it, she thought absently, cradling his hand between both of her own. The shock of feeling his skin warm against hers pulsed through her bloodstream. His fingertips were rough, just as she'd imagined. There were traces of dirt in the creases of his knuckles, probably from digging around in the mulch. His hand looked twice as big as hers, but maybe her perceptions were altered by the unique experience of touching her forbidden fantasy man in the flesh. Indeed, her head seemed lighter than air, floating six inches above the rest of her body.

Her voice murmured distantly. "We can get to know each other, and then, if that works out..." It would; instinctively, she knew it would. "We'll finalize the... arrangement." *Wow.* If she'd known that this was what an arranged marriage could be, she'd have been a supporter of Grandmother's campaign right from the start!

"Are you a palm reader?" Jed asked gruffly.

"What?" The question had flustered her. "No."

"Then can I have my hand back?"

She dropped it immediately. "I'm sorry." She cringed inside. "I've been presumptuous." A first, that.

"No problem." His voice was as raspy as a cheap piece of sandpaper and it was rubbing her all the right ways. "That is, if you mean I'm hired."

"Hired! What a way of putting it!"

Jed folded his arms across his chest. "So we're back to the trial period?"

"Yes." Gussy frowned. There was *definitely* something amiss. It sounded almost like Jed was applying for a job. Her gaze dropped to his work boots again. Okay, so he wasn't as well off as the majority of her suitors, but really, did he think she was going to *pay* him to marry her?

Gussy froze. Oh, no. What if he was a fortune hunter? Or, dare she think it, a gigolo?

"We can get together later then," Jed was saying, "after I've finished moving my stuff into the carriage house."

"You're moving in?" Gussy squeaked. The mouse was back.

"Yeah." Jed headed for the side door that opened directly onto the north terrace. "I was looking for a place to rent, and since your carriage house was empty, Mrs. Throckmorton said I might as well take it for convenience's sake. I'll be around so much, anyway..." He shrugged.

Gussy was trying to assimilate all that he'd said and having a tough time at it. Grandmother had approved of Jed Kelley so much she was letting him move into the carriage house?

No way.

"You have a problem with that, Miss Fairchild?" Jed asked, halfway out the door.

"I...no, I suppose not." What else could even the new Gussy say? Apparently it had already been "arranged" without the intended's knowledge or consent!

"Fine." He flipped his hand at her. "See you later."

Gussy moved to one of the unshaded windows to watch him cross the lawn in long, athletic strides. She was trembling all over like a malaria victim in a snowstorm, shot with hot charges and cold shivers until her brain was numb. This couldn't be true, could it?

Fantasy men didn't happen to mice like her.

TEN MINUTES LATER, having gained some control over her extremities, Gussy stumbled into the library. Grandmother could always be found at her desk at this hour of the morning, efficiently seeing to the paperwork of running the estate and dispatching luncheon invitations or courteous thank-you notes on Throckmorton Cottage letterhead.

"Grandmother."

Marian held up one finger for silence as she blotted the ink of her fountain pen and then ripped the check she'd completed out of the household ledger. After depositing the check in an envelope and using a small damp sponge to seal the flap and apply a stamp, she finally peered at her granddaughter over the top of her half-moon reading glasses. "What is it, Augustina?"

Gussy dropped onto a cracked, oxblood-leather ottoman and hugged her knees, wishing this wasn't the first day of the rest of her life so she could fold up like an accordion and whimper with hankering distress.

"Jed Kelley," she croaked.

"Ah, you've met with him, then?"

So it was true. Not knowing if she should cheer or swoon, Gussy just nodded dumbly.

"I meant to tell you about Mr. Kelley at breakfast," Marian continued offhandedly, "but you were in too much of a rush and I'm afraid I didn't get the chance."

Grandmother was like that. Now that Gussy was nominally an adult she couldn't be actually punished for her transgressions, but she could be reminded of them with neat little bloodless zingers that always found their mark. This time, the new Gussy actually said in response, "Kind of a big deal to overlook."

Marian slipped off her glasses. "Oh, dear. I *do* hope I haven't inconvenienced you, Augustina." Her stare would normally have pierced Gussy's self-confidence; today, sharper daggers than one of her grandmother's looks were already needling Gussy with worry.

Holding herself tightly, she rocked to and fro on the ottoman. "Please tell me about him, Grandmother. I don't understand how—how you..."

Marian turned to a stack of correspondence. "While I admit it was a snap decision, I've learned to trust my instincts about these things. Mr. Kelley will do nicely."

Do what nicely? Gussy wailed inside. *Marry your unmarriageable granddaughter? Abscond with her Throckmorton trust fund?*

"But what about Andrews?" she asked miserably. Andrews had been Grandmother's grandson-in-law front-runner for years; surely he hadn't fallen out of the race since breakfast without Gussy being aware of it.

Marian was reading a note from her daughter in France.

Nathalie and Philip would be in residence at their villa in Provence until August, when perhaps they'd fly to Maine to escape the heat. "I don't see what Andrews has to do with it. The Lowells already have an excellent man. Mr. Kelley was recommended by both Bibi Lightford and Vanessa Van Pelt." She frowned and flipped through a folder from one of the compartments of her rolltop desk. "Not that I'd employ anyone on Vanessa's ill-advised word, but his very fine references checked out as well and he seemed quite knowledgeable. I know I have his résumé here somewhere."

Gussy bolted upright. "What?"

"Spare me the screeching, Augustina. You know how sensitive my ears are."

Gussy's face was as pale as milk and for once she forgot her pardon-me-ma'ams. "Jed Kelley…"

"Here it is." Marian held up the paper-clipped résumé.

"Jed Kelley…" Gussy whispered.

Either blasé or blind to her granddaughter's response, Marian handed Gussy the papers. "Yes," she said with complete confidence, "Mr. Jed Kelley will do very well as our new gardener."

GRUNTING AND HEAVING and remembering to lift with his legs and not his back, Jed hefted the next-to-last moving box out of the bed of his brand-new fire-engine red pickup truck. Had to be books, he thought, staggering through the open door of the carriage house and up the steps. Nothing was as heavy as books.

He set the box on the floor by the built-in bookshelves flanking the living room's small fireplace. As long as he was bent over anyway, he paused to rub at the twinges of pain in his right knee. Lifting with your legs was all well and good for someone with two good knees, but for a gimpy-legged ex-hockey player like Jed it was a surefire prescription for a late date with the liniment bottle.

Aw, well, what the hell. At least the liniment would do him some good, unlike the sweet-smelling feminine kind of late date he'd once preferred.

Jed straightened and walked over to the dormer window that faced Throckmorton Cottage. It was not a cottage in any way, shape or form. It was a classic mid-1850s manor house, big, square, solid, Greek Revival probably, constructed of tawny pink brick and trimmed in white, with black-green shutters. The formal gardens were so extensive Jed would have to hire additional help to keep up with the demands of both this job and the others he'd lined up for his fledgling landscape-and-garden-design business.

He hoped that this flighty Gussy person, the amorous heiress, as he'd already begun to think of her, wouldn't interfere overmuch in his work around the Throckmorton estate. At the previous week's interview, Mrs. Throckmorton had explained about Miss Fairchild's Vassar degree in botany and how she would be overseeing Jed's work. Jed had gotten the feeling that Miss Fairchild's authority was nominal at best—who'd been interviewing him, after all?—and that she was probably one of those throwback Ivy League dilettantes occupying herself until marriage by dabbling in gardening, needlepoint and the occasional spot of charity work.

Meeting Gussy hadn't exactly changed his mind. Meeting her beaux, those two lapdogs dressed in tennis togs and sailing gear, had only reinforced the assumption.

Still, Jed had to admit that she was sort of pretty. Her kind usually were, although she wasn't quite the pampered, glossy beauty he'd halfway expected. Actually, he'd figured on either a glamour girl or a limp-haired wallflower wearing rumpled chinos and gum boots, with several dogs dancing attendance at her heels. Gussy Fairchild had been neither...or maybe a little bit of both.

Jed shrugged and stumped back down the narrow stairway for the last box. Either way you looked at it, this Gussy person definitely had a screw loose. The way she'd cooed nonsense at him, shimmied her hips and caressed his hand had been at best an unconventional approach to their initial consultation. Not as blatant as Vanessa Van Pelt's behavior, but certainly an overly amorous way to treat the new gardener.

"Rich society chicks," Jed said, scooping up a box so light it had to contain his kitchen supplies. "Whaddya gonna do?"

Get used to it, he answered himself. There'd be no avoiding working with them. Apparently he'd have to get used to fending them off, too.

Jed was not the kind of man who would happily reap his own physical satisfaction by allowing himself to be used by amorous heiresses with idle minds and restless hands. No way. No matter how soft and pink as dew-kissed roses were their lips.

And now that that was settled, he could quit thinking about the dishonorable Miss Augustina Fairchild, right? *Right*.

Glad he'd had the barber give him a zip cut in preparation for a hot summer of outdoor work, Jed swiped his sleeve across his forehead as he passed the old wooden carriage doors that opened to a converted garage containing a vintage Silver Cloud Rolls-Royce and a more practical midnight blue coupe. Since the oozy butler up at the main house had already informed Jed that the Throckmortons no longer employed a chauffeur, Jed was hoping that he wouldn't be expected to ferry the cars between here and there. If he was going to make a success of his new busi-

ness, he couldn't afford the time to be at the beck and call
of the Throckmortons.

Living on the estate could be a problem, he realized.
Mrs. Throckmorton wasn't the type to demand service; she
was the type who *expected* it. And Gussy was the type
who… Well, he was no longer absolutely sure of what type
Gussy was. She had suitors lined up at the door and her
manner was flirtatious, but there'd also been that moment
when she'd first squinted through the glare and said hello,
looking for all the world like a timid little mouse expecting
a rebuff.

Jeez. He really had to get her off his mind.

The door to the second-floor apartment was shrouded
with lush climbing ivy; Jed left it open behind him so fresh
air would circulate throughout his new living quarters,
which were about as different from the sleek, spacious,
impersonal condo he still owned in Hartford as a guy could
get. Even though someone had recently dusted and polished, the four furnished rooms had retained a faint,
closed-up, unused mustiness. The space was on the small
side, with unexpected nooks, patterned Victorian wallpaper
faded to pastels and low, slanted ceilings that opened into
ivy-hung dormers, one in each room. The branches of the
towering pines and firs that sheltered the brick carriage
house brushed at its windows and roofs each time the wind
gusted, a pleasant sound in counterpoint to the distant
swish of the surf.

After depositing the last box in the tiny kitchen, Jed got
a long-necked beer from the fridge and returned to the
mullioned window in the living room's dormer. He stared
at the main house, thinking that to keep all that boxwood
clipped would be practically a part-time job all on its own.
He cranked the window open to the refreshing salt air, then

forgot his beer on the sill when he went to wash up. His knee joint had begun to loosen up; he hardly limped at all.

He had his shirt off, the water running and his face lathered when a feminine voice called from the upper landing. "Hello? Mr. Kelley? Are you home?"

Jed splashed cold water on his face and grabbed a towel from a stack he'd just unpacked. Swabbing runnels of soapy water off his bare chest, he walked into the living room and found the amorous heiress herself standing uneasily at the open door, her feet still out on the landing but her head and shoulders poked past the jamb. She flinched and pulled back when she saw him.

"Jed," he said. "Call me Jed."

She stared at his chest, her shiny eyes as round and brown as old copper pennies.

The corners of Jed's mouth twitched; he draped the towel around his neck. "It's Augustina, am I right?"

She managed a nod. "Uh-huh."

"Come on in, Augustina," he invited, but she didn't budge an inch. In fact, she looked ready to bolt. Not the seductress he'd met up at the house, he thought. Same body, though, shown off to slender advantage by the clinging halter top of her pale-pink flowered dress. Her bare shoulders looked as smooth and tasty as sweet buttercream frosting.

"I prefer Gussy," she blurted.

"Unusual name."

She licked her lips. "My parents named each of their daughters after the month of their birth. Since I'm not the Tina type, and Augie is even worse than Gussy..." She shrugged, her gaze glued to his biceps, and asked with a sweet little breathy moan, "Is that a tattoo?"

"Yes, that would be a tattoo." Jed was grinning openly now. The tattoo was an ugly thing, a ferocious black bear.

"One of those drunk-on-school-spirit-and-a-kegger decisions I've since lived to regret."

She was staring at the tattoo as if she'd never seen one before. Maybe she hadn't. Her dozens of boyfriends probably weren't the type, unless Harvard had changed a hell of a lot since Jed's team used to bodycheck theirs right off the ice. "I played college hockey at the University of Maine," he elaborated. "The Black Bears, you know."

Progress: she blinked.

Jed could handle her reaction. Having played professional hockey for six years, he'd met his share of impressionable, shiny-eyed sports groupies. And the harder-edged, bleached-blond camp followers, too, the type of women his more callous teammates had used and discarded at their convenience. Then there was the third type, the pretty, sweet and to all appearances sincere girls who took a guy's engagement ring when he was up and threw it in his face when he was down, the girls whose seemingly genuine love masked the reality of their mercenary, status-grubbing souls.

Of course, an heiress like Gussy didn't have to play in that league. She wasn't going to be impressed by money or fancy cars—good thing, since he'd just traded in his Porsche. The acclaim and privilege of his star-athlete status, while irrevocably defunct, probably wouldn't have been worth peanuts in her crowd, either.

She was still staring.

Jed supposed it was possible that Gussy's awed reaction was in response to his gaucherie at appearing bare-chested before the lady of the manor, junior version. But somehow he doubted it.

Nope. It had to be his sheer masculine pulchritude she was reacting to with such a faltering fascination.

Which was kind of funny, now that he thought of it, coming from a supposed flirt like the amorous heiress here.

A big dog bounded into the room, breaking up their tableau. It sniffed the air, barked once at Jed, wagged its tail at his answering smile and lunged without warning, planting its paws on his chest and enthusiastically swiping its tongue across his face.

"Percy, down," commanded Gussy.

Laughing, Jed put his hands around the beast's upper body and tried to push it away. The dog's cold nose nuzzled his neck as it slurped behind his ear.

Gussy grabbed Percy's collar and hauled him off Jed. "I'm so sorry. Percy is sometimes too exuberant to obey my commands."

Jed looked at the stolid golden retriever, sitting on its haunches, pink tongue lolling, feathered tail sweeping the floor in friendly arcs. "At least he likes me."

Gussy bent at the waist and murmured something to the dog as she smoothed its fur beneath the collar. Her long brown hair slipped across her cheek and the filtered sunshine from the window burnished it to a rich, molten, golden-brown flow of honey that was only a shade or two darker than Percy's fur. She straightened, flipping her hair back from the headband, and he saw that her eyes, too, were the same as the dog's: a glistening velvety brown lashed in dark gold, wide with eagerness and a slight anxiety.

In the dog's case the eager anxiety came from wanting to be released to attack Jed's face with its tongue. As for Gussy...he didn't know.

Maybe the same. Or so a man could hope.

No, jeez, no, not that, he thought, thoroughly frustrated with himself. He wasn't supposed to be ready for another relationship. Not even a bucolic D. H. Lawrence–inspired romp, with Gussy as Lady Chatterley and himself as the gamekeeper.

Especially not that.

"Percy likes everyone," Gussy said. "He's very friendly."

And so was she, Jed reminded himself, thinking of her accumulation of lovesick admirers. "Then he won't be attacking me unawares among the azaleas?"

Her smile was shy. "Not viciously, anyway. Though I can't promise good behavior."

"That's okay. I don't mind muddy paw prints on my work clothes."

Gussy's glance touched on his chest, then bounced away. "Is the apartment all right? It can get hot up here in the summertime." She was staring at the moving boxes, trying hard not to look at him. "If I'd known you were coming, I'd have fixed it up a little. Stocked the refrigerator, arranged flowers, that sort of thing."

"It's fine." He considered what she'd said, then added, "You didn't know I was coming?" And if not, then whom had she thought she was talking to so coquettishly, back there in the solarium?

"Umm...there was a small miscommunication between me and my grandmother about hiring a new gardener, that's all."

"Oh?"

She blushed. "I—I'm sorry if I gave you the wrong impression. Before, I mean. Holding your ha—" She stopped her halting speech by biting her lip. "What I'm trying to say is that you're hired. Officially."

"No trial period?"

She shook her head, forming a silent *no* with her lips.

He could have kissed her then, but he held himself in check. If Gussy's initial behavior toward him had been overly amorous, then who knew what his kissing her would qualify him for—except possibly unemployment. Which he couldn't afford, if not in terms of money, then in what it would cost his reputation. He wasn't interested in being the permanent stud-muffin gardener to the Vanessa Van Pelts of the world.

"Well, that's good," he said. Percy snuffled around the boxes, his toenails clicking on the oak plank floor.

"So...I hope you'll like it here." Gussy edged toward the door.

Jed found that he wanted her to stay. "Can I get you a drink?" He snatched his beer bottle off the windowsill. "I don't suppose you drink beer?"

She looked down at her clasped hands. "Water?"

"Okay, water," he said. "Wait here." He turned toward the kitchen, the dog at his heels, then spun back and grabbed a garment bag and his answering machine off a worn, green-velvet love seat. "Make yourself comfortable."

When he came back with the glass of water, Gussy was still standing, though she'd moved to the window and was looking past the interwoven evergreen branches to the large brick house on the rise. She took the water with a murmured "Thanks," and drank it down without pause, dutifully, then handed the empty glass back to him. He waited. Her big eyes swiveled toward him at last and her lips slowly parted, but all she said was, "Percy?"

As the dog trotted into the room, licking his chops, Jed told himself he wasn't disappointed. He had to remember that his so-called masculine pulchritude wouldn't go as far now that he was no longer a big-deal pro athlete, and that was probably a good thing.

Besides, to Gussy he was just a gardener. She was obviously embarrassed about whatever had been going on in the solarium; she could scarcely bear to look him in the eye. Which meant that it wasn't likely she'd ever see him for the man he was inside.

Not unlike his fickle former fiancée.

"We've bothered you long enough," Gussy said, snapping her fingers at Percy as she walked to the doorway. Once there, she put one hand on the jamb and paused, her back to Jed. Her straight, golden-brown hair fell smoothly to just above her shoulder blades, leaving much of her lovely back bare, literally so luscious in its butter-cream perfection that his mouth watered.

He saw her rib cage expand as she took a deep breath. "Since it's your first day at Throckmorton Cottage..." she hesitated, then glanced over her shoulder "...why don't you come up to the house for dinner this evening?" Percy also looked back, his tail weaving from side to side.

Jed cleared his throat, hesitating.

"Grandmother will be there, of course. I'm sure she'd be delighted to have you."

Oh, I'm sure.

"We can discuss your work in the garden."

Yup. The garden.

"Our latest French chef quit in a snit, but the housekeeper who's filling in is an adequate cook. You won't go hungry, and there's apple tart for dessert."

"Okay, you've convinced me," Jed said, smiling, though he was still waiting for Gussy to mention her own delight in having him. If one could call it that. "I'll be there. I'll even put on a shirt."

She smiled hugely, said a breathless goodbye and fairly galloped down the stairs, the dog bounding joyously at her heels.

After a minute, Jed wandered back to the bathroom, his hands knotted on the towel around his neck. Dinner at the big house, with the formidable Mrs. Throckmorton quizzing him on his theories about hybrids and making notes on his table manners, sounded like fun.

So why was his face in the mirror grinning like a hyena? Jed shook his head and reached for the soap. No soap. He looked in the sink, then at the haphazardly scattered towels he'd thought he'd left in a neat stack on the commode. Maybe he'd knocked them over without realizing it, but still, where was the soap?

He shook out the towels, found nothing, and even traced his route into the living room and back again. No soap.

Odd. He thought of Gussy, alone for a moment while he was in the kitchen, and operating under the influence of a masculine pulchritude that maybe wasn't as diminished as he'd assumed, then concluded, no, of course not. What could Gussy possibly want with his soap?

Dismissing the matter as yet another unsolved mystery, he rummaged around in a box until he found another of the skimpy hotel soaps he'd collected from one too many road games and then went back to washing up, watching his ridiculous grinning face in the mirror.

He really was going to have to stop thinking about Gussy as anything other than his boss.

Starting tomorrow.

3

Dinner with the Throckmortons

To CORRECT the mistaken impression she'd given Jed in the solarium—she had to, didn't she, since he certainly couldn't go on thinking of her as a flirt…?—Gussy had dressed for dinner like a nun on holiday, in a cream organza blouse with a multilayered collar of fluted ruffles, a plain shin-length navy blue skirt, patterned ivory stockings and slip-on flats with neat blue grosgrain bows. She'd made herself wear the round wire-rimmed glasses and had parted her hair in the middle. If she didn't look quite like a nun, then she looked like the most virtuous of novitiates.

Jed looked like a male animal, even in his tailored suit and muted silk tie. Forcing her gaze away from him before the hunger in her eyes betrayed her, Gussy responded in a monotone to something Andrews had said about the regatta next Saturday. Andrews, of course, looked like Andrews: flat blond hair, pale blue eyes, aquiline nose and mushy chin, wearing a Harvard club tie and a navy blazer with some sort of *Mayflower* crest on the pocket.

Grandmother Throckmorton had invited Andrews to dinner, independent of Gussy inviting Jed. An initially unpleasant surprise, but perhaps all for the best.

After Gussy had discovered that Jed was a gardener and not one of her network of reluctant admirers—a realization that still made her cringe—she'd wasted no time in dis-

carding the impulsive idea about using marriage to free
herself from the Throckmorton restraints. Not that he'd
ask, but marrying Jed would cause more upheaval than
even a solo declaration of independence, so that meant her
best remaining prospect was Andrews. And marrying Andrews was strictly a last resort. Although she'd gain some
measure of respect and freedom as Mrs. Andrews Lowell,
their benefit would be limited. Gussy would still be stuck
in Sheepshead Bay, expected to conform to the rules of
respectable young matronhood. She wasn't ready for that.
Especially not after meeting Jed.

His becoming forbidden fruit had only made her want
him more—and she wasn't about to analyze the psychological ramifications of *that.*

Once Grandmother had concluded her recycled garden-
club lecture on *Rosa rugosas,* to which Jed had nodded
compliantly but withheld most comment, Andrews began
questioning Jed about his hockey career. It seemed that
Andrews had actually played hockey himself and was trying to assert that the Harvard club team was nearly as good
as their NCAA team, to which Jed withheld both com-
ments and nods. Every now and then his gaze would flick
briefly over Gussy; each time she felt the jolt of his sizzling, electric blue eyes.

"I played field hockey at Miss Fibbing-White's," she
announced at a lull in the conversation. "Ugh. Big,
healthy, horsey girls in plaid skirts and knee socks. Phoebe
Beecham was very nasty with the stick. My shins were
black-and-blue for an entire semester."

Ignoring her contribution as frivolous, Andrews asked
Jed with some suspicion, "For which team did you play?
I don't recall your name."

Like Andrews was an expert, Gussy thought.

"The Black Wings, then the Whalers. Six years alto-

gether, until I was blindsided by Howitzer O'Hallihan during a road game and wrecked my knee and my eye.''

Gussy winced in sympathy. "Is that how you got the
scar?''

"What scar?'' Andrews said.

Jed didn't respond immediately, which made Gussy vac-
illate. "I'm sorry. Was that rude of me to ask?'' At the
head of the table, Grandmother shook her head slightly, so
Gussy supposed it was.

Truth be known, she found Jed's scar extremely attractive. He looked like a pirate, or maybe a desperado. Sort
of dashing, and possibly dangerous, the kind of man who
made his enemies' blood run cold and a lady's run hot.

"Let's skip the medical report,'' Jed replied. "It's
enough to say that between the knee and the eye injury, I
took early retirement.''

"In that case, how fortunate for you that athletes are
paid such overblown salaries,'' Andrews sniped, and
Gussy realized that he must be feeling competitive with
Jed, and also jealous, because otherwise he'd never have
mentioned money at the dinner table. She was surprised;
she hadn't thought that Andrews cared enough to be jealous.

"I didn't have a superstar contract,'' Jed said quietly,
"but I was paid very well, yes.''

Andrews's bland face stayed bland even as he said,
"Then mucking about in gardens must be quite a comedown.''

Jed went very still.

Timing her interruption impeccably, Marian made a pro-
duction out of ringing for Thwaite to remove the soup
plates and bring in the main course. They were having
Cornish game hens.

In the oppressive silence, the butler took the platter of

crisp, golden-brown fowl around the table. When it was Gussy's turn, he removed the tray just quickly enough to make her spatter hot drippings on the tablecloth. Grandmother's lips tightened. While Thwaite made a show of swabbing at the mess, Gussy ducked her chin and mumbled a "Pardon me, ma'am," to the pearl buttons of her blouse.

Jed averted attention by asking pointedly, "And what do you do, Andrews?"

Andrews blustered about scouting new investments and the hassle of keeping up his portfolio, trying to make it sound like a full-time job. Gussy knew that he'd briefly been an investment banker until he'd come into a smallish inheritance from a great-uncle and had retired to devote all his time to building the windfall into a fortune. Although naturally it wasn't spoken of in polite company, the Sheepshead Bay Lowells' finances had taken a downturn in recent years. And since it wasn't spoken of, Gussy could not be *entirely* certain that Grandmother's motives in marrying her to Andrews were for reasons of providing the Lowells with a welcome cash transfusion. But the possibility had occurred to her.

Gussy pushed the poor little dead hen to the far side of her plate and nibbled at the vegetables, thinking that it would now be hypocritical of her to complain about Grandmother's motives. Marrying for practical monetary reasons was not much different than her own plan to marry for independence. Even though the plan had been short-lived, she might have actually gone through with it, if...

If only Jed were half as acceptable to the Throckmortons as Andrews.

But then he wouldn't be Jed. And his being Jed—Gussy watched beneath her lashes as he neatly dissected the bird's carcass and still kept up his end of the conversation with throwaway aplomb—his being Jed was exactly what she liked about him.

It wasn't only his tattoo or his magnificent physique that she was attracted to—but while she was on the subject, be still her beating heart. It was also the rest of him, the inside of him. He seemed intelligent, good-humored and quietly in control. He hadn't had to get all macho and huffed-up over Andrews's childish put-downs or her own schoolgirl goggling. Nor had he taken any guff from Thwaite, who could smell vulnerability a mile away and pounced on it mercilessly once he'd sniffed it out. In fact, Gussy was waiting with interest to see what kind of working association Jed might establish with Grandmother. If she was reading his strength of character right, it could be the clash of the titans.

In short, Jed Kelley was a man who knew what he was about.

No wonder she, the pusillanimouse, liked him so much.

And no wonder their relationship was doomed. Andrews was the sort of wishy-washy man she deserved and would probably wind up with. And while that likelihood had always frustrated her, it was now producing an actual pang in the area of her heart.

"When can you make up that tennis match we missed this morning, Gussy?" Andrews asked. "Felicity and Ted want to play doubles."

Felicity was hideous and Ted was a bore, but Grandmother was listening, so Gussy smiled vivaciously and arranged a date. Pusillanimice who didn't dare speak up got what they deserved.

Across the table, Jed seethed. Dinner with the Throckmortons was even worse than he'd imagined, not so much because of the evil-eyed butler or Marian Throckmorton's off-the-starched-cuff gardening lecture, but because it meant that he had to sit and watch while Gussy flirted with her boyfriend. Make that one of her boyfriends.

Suffering in silence, Jed had watched while she'd smiled and chatted and once even touched Andrews's sleeve. Now she was making a date.

Of course, he had no call to object. She'd flirted with him a little, yeah. Since when had flirting meant anything special? It was becoming clear that such behavior was a matter of course with the amorous heiress.

Marian was also watching, but with doting approval. "What are you doing for the regatta, Andrews?"

"We were discussing that earlier. I won't be racing this year, so I'll watch from Felicity and Ted's porch, since they have the best view," Andrews said. Jed found his rival's lofty self-satisfaction irritating. "Would you care to join me, Gussy? And for the dance later?"

"I've promised to sell drinks at the garden club's refreshment booth," Gussy said, sounding breathless.

"You're free for the dance," Marian prodded.

Gussy released a held breath and let her eyes blink shut for a moment of what to Jed looked like vexation. Maybe Andrews wasn't her first choice, he thought with a pleasure that instantly turned to dismay at the possibility that followed: or she already had an even hotter date lined up.

"Yes, I'd be delighted to go to the dance with you," Gussy said to Andrews, though her gaze seemed to linger on Jed.

Andrews shot a look of triumph across the table. Jed found him easy to ignore. Tilting back his head, he narrowed his eyes to focus on Gussy alone. She looked like an angel in the diffused, refracted light of the chandelier, all soft creams and gentle pinks, with golden sparks glancing off her schoolmarm glasses and the sheen of her hair. He felt the tugging heat of his physical reaction, and worse, the treacherous warming of his heart. Damn. If she'd had the brittle, sophisticated beauty of a proper femme fatale, all this could have been easily avoided. Instead she seemed sweet and kind and unexpectedly vulnerable—just the kind of girl he liked best. Still, all that might be part of her come-on. He was a sap for wanting her.

"The Sheepshead Bay regatta is quite a sight, Mr. Kelley." Marian was expansive now that she'd arranged her granddaughter's schedule to suit herself. "Most of us make a day of it."

"I expect I'll be working, Mrs. Throckmorton," Jed replied dryly. He was going to be putting in full days even on the weekends for at least the foreseeable future.

"Really, you must squeeze in a moment to stop by the harbor." Marian surveyed the table and rang for Thwaite to clear. "The races continue all afternoon."

"You could buy a glass of lemonade to support the garden club," Gussy put in softly.

He looked across the table at her and smiled. "Maybe I'll do that."

"There are other amusements, as well," Marian continued smoothly. "A pie-eating contest, the Sisterhood's quilting exhibition and of course the garden show. Beatrice Hyde's floribundas are traditionally magnificent. I'd love to learn her secret, but she's much too crotchety to comply."

"And if you don't like lemonade, there's a beer tent." Andrews dug into the tart Thwaite had just served.

"I like lemonade fine," Jed replied. "After a hard morning's work trimming Mrs. Van Pelt's hedges and climbing vines, I may be wrung out enough to drink a gallon of it."

A short, surprised huff of laughter burst from Andrews's

full mouth as he hastily covered it with a napkin. Gussy's eyes darkened mysteriously before she averted her gaze from Jed's, resolutely refusing to look up.

"I think I mentioned before that Mrs. Van Pelt is one of the clients of my new business," Jed said into the awkward silence. Damned if he knew why they all looked like they'd just swallowed marbles.

Marian Throckmorton cleared her throat. "Be that as it may," she said pompously, then stopped flat.

Gussy was studying her dessert plate as if it were the Rosetta stone. Andrews held the napkin over his mouth and chewed, his cheeks ruddy.

Jed took a cursory sip of coffee, a bite of the apple tart, and decided that he'd had enough. If he was going to play the outsider, he'd prefer to be literally outside rather than sitting around a table with these stuffy prigs. He glanced once more at Gussy; her only response was the tiniest flicker of her gold-tipped eyelashes.

"Thanks for dinner, Mrs. Throckmorton," he said, standing. Gussy's head jerked up. "It's been swell and all, but I've got a full day tomorrow."

"Augustina and I shall see you in the morning for our tour of the garden, as arranged," Marian replied. "Good evening, Mr. Kelley."

Gussy popped to her feet. "But—"

"Sit down, Augustina." Marian gestured for the butler. "Thwaite will show Mr. Kelley out."

Gussy sank back down.

"Goodness," Marian said once Jed and the butler had departed.

"Trimming Mrs. V.P.'s hedges," Andrews snorted. Gussy gnawed gently on her lip, her hands clenched in her lap.

Marian picked up her fork. "What can one expect from—"

Gussy jumped up, arms stiff, fists at her side. "You're both terribly rude!"

She ran headlong from the dining room after Jed and collided directly with Thwaite in the hall. He tottered backward, and she grabbed his forearms to keep him from falling, finding them astonishingly frail. The fleeting thought occurred to her that Thwaite was only a sour old man, not someone to be intimidated by, but then she was flying through the front hall and throwing open the heavy wooden door, calling anxiously for Jed.

A bulky shadow loomed before her.

"Oh, Jed," she panted, putting out her hands. She felt massive, bunched muscles shifting beneath cold bare skin. For an instant the light from the open doorway shone on a hairless pate and then the shadowed bulk stepped closer, illuminating a monstrous, glowering face with hairy black brows, beady eyes and mangled skin. It was a horrific visage.

Gussy screamed.

4

Dessert with Gussy

JED HAD CUT ACROSS the dark expanse of parkway and was almost to the carriage house when he heard a woman scream. Gussy, he knew in an instant, and before a conscious decision was made he was racing back to the main house across the velvety lawn, leaping the balustrade of the terrace wall without breaking stride. *Gussy.*

Thwaite, Marian, Andrews and Jed all arrived at once, in a flurry of tremulous excitement and exclamations. Marian's voice rose above the clamor. "What is the meaning of all this shrieking, Augustina?"

Gussy emerged from the shadows at the bottom of the steps, towing a man—a strange, massive, hulking man with a bald head. "It's Godfrey," she said.

Marian fanned herself with a lace-edged handkerchief. "Godfrey? We certainly don't know anyone named Godfrey."

Jed stepped closer. Godfrey was six-two, at least, and all muscle. He was wearing a see-through red net T-shirt and tight black leather pants, and he was the ugliest man Jed had ever seen. Gussy's hand had to curve *way* around his biceps and his triceps in order to tug him up the stone steps.

"He's April's butler," she explained. "I ran into him in the dark."

Thwaite sniffed in snooty dismissal. Godfrey glared until the other butler recoiled, shrinking back against the white columns that supported the elaborate portico above the entrance. Jed decided that maybe looks weren't everything.

"Why in the world is he here in Maine?" Marian demanded. "April is on her honeymoon."

"I gather that he's just finished closing up April's house in Chicago, since she and her new husband will be going straight on to Guatemala after the honeymoon." Gussy patted Godfrey's thick arm. "April told him that we'd put him up at Throckmorton Cottage until he leaves for England."

"England? Goodness." After a trenchant pause, Marian conceded, "I suppose we can let him stay the night and then secure a seat on an airplane first thing tomorrow. Now, let's all get out of this chilly night air, shall we?" The group began to move inside. "Thwaite, place a call to my travel agent in the morn—"

"I don't fly."

The accent was British, the tone gruff. Everyone stopped and looked back at Godfrey, who stood unmoving and once again silent, his only baggage the lumpy duffel slung across his wide shoulders.

"You don't fly?" Gussy prompted.

"Never," Godfrey grunted.

"Then…?"

Godfrey's black brows knitted beneath his bulging forehead, making him look even more foul-tempered. "April gave me a ticket for the *QE II.* It sails in five weeks."

Marian made a sound of exclamation and tossed up her hands in surrender. Taking Andrews's arm, she marched inside, her voice trailing behind her. "What *will* April think of next.…"

"Welcome to Throckmorton Cottage," Gussy said to Godfrey. "I hope you'll enjoy your stay." She prodded him toward the door, where Thwaite stood holding it open, his pale, lined face a frozen mask of dislike. "Go on inside, Godfrey. Thwaite will be glad to fix you up, won't you, Thwaite?"

"As you wish, Miss Augustina."

"Are you coming, Gussy?" Andrews called from the front hall.

She looked at Jed. "In a minute." Once the door was closed, she added in a soft voice, "After I walk Jed back to the carriage house."

Smiling, Jed shook his head. "Do you think I'm going to send you back all alone in the dark? One bloodcurdling scream in the night is about all I can take."

"You'd have screamed, too, if you'd grabbed hold of Godfrey in the dark," she protested. "But, really, Jed, I don't make a habit of screaming. And I'm familiar with every blade of grass on this estate, so I should be safe as houses."

"Halfway?" he compromised. "A nice moonlit stroll as far as the fountain?"

"Yes," she agreed, her voice fading to a tender, sibilant sigh as she took Jed's arm with more caution than she had Godfrey's. They left the arc of bright light at the door and followed the silvery path lit by softly glowing minibulbs placed near the ground, their footsteps crunching on the gravel. The only other sounds were the trickling splashes of the fountain ahead of them and the rush and swish of the ocean behind.

Jed broke their silence. "So who is this April person and what compelled her to hire a man like Godfrey as her butler?"

Gussy laughed. "April is my older sister, by two years.

She recently remarried, to an archaeologist who works in Central America. I don't know exactly why she hired Godfrey, but I think I'm going to like him. She's told me he's not as ferocious as he looks."

Jed added his chuckle to hers. "One can only hope."

"It will do Thwaite some good to be challenged for a change." Gussy paused thoughtfully; Jed could almost hear the ratcheting of the gears in her head. "I don't know why I'm such a ninny, but Thwaite has always intimidated me."

"Only because you let him." *And your grandmother, too,* he thought. Strange how she was so meek with Mrs. Throckmorton and Thwaite, yet so openly flirtatious with her male admirers. Was it possible that he'd been wrong about her? Was she not a capricious, amorous heiress, after all?

They passed the bulbous, black-green shapes of the topiary and came to the circular court where the gravel paths converged. The pool of the small fountain was lit below the surface of the water, producing an effect of weaving liquid light and shadow that bathed Gussy's oval face with chiaroscuro when she stopped and turned to look up at Jed.

Wearing the glasses, she was pretty in an open, ordinary way, he decided, her even features pleasant but certainly not stunning. It was the depth of her big brown eyes that drew him, and the succulent temptation of her richly pink lips. Yet one question still made him cautious. Was she as genuine as she now appeared?

"You confuse me," he confessed.

She seemed delighted. "I do?"

"I never know quite what to expect from you."

How marvelous, Gussy almost blurted. She'd always been so quiet and unassuming, forever backstage compared to the limelight lives led by April and their parents. Although up to now she'd thought her decision to run her own show had been a miserable failure, perhaps it wasn't…entirely.

Jed had noticed her. Jed was really *seeing* her.

She snatched off her glasses.

But what next? What would April, for instance, do at a moment like this?

"I'm sorry you missed dessert," Gussy whispered.

"Yeah, well, I sort of got the feeling that I'd said something wrong."

She didn't want to explain about Vanessa Van Pelt and her penchant for sleeping with her gardeners, not when a similar notion had seized Gussy's own mind. Strangely, even that delighted her. No one in all of Sheepshead Bay would believe that Gussy Gutless actually had something in common with Vanessa Van Vixen.

She shifted nervously. "Still, I'd like to make it up to you."

Jed cocked one brow and the thin white scar moved with it, crinkling the skin at the outer corner of his eye. "Did you have something in mind?"

Did she ever. *Do it,* she thought. *Do it.*

Before she could chicken out, Gussy threw her arms around his neck. "Sweets for the sweet," she said, and started kissing him. Her ardor was enthusiastic but awkward; she wasn't very good at this type of thing.

Jed brought both his hands up to the middle of her back, then let one of them creep higher until it cupped the back of her head. His touch gentled her frantic motions and she started to relax a little, slipping back to her heels in the security of his strong arms. The desire that had been coiled in her belly began its long, slow unfurling. The tingling heat of it seeped into her bones.

His hand twisted in her thick hair, making her head tilt to one side. Suddenly, with one small, sexy, sliding adjustment, their lips fit together and the kiss was right. Absolutely, deliciously right.

"How..." Gussy murmured, but Jed's warm mouth closed again over her lips and then she didn't care. She only wanted to kiss him, kiss him until the sky fell and the waves washed over them and the world came to an end, because for just this one moment in time, she was a star, a brilliant celestial body, and it was far more wonderful than she'd ever dared dream.

Perhaps all that was asking too much of a kiss. As abruptly as she'd thrown herself at him, Jed dropped his arms and stepped away. Feeling dazed, as if she'd been struck by lightning and left standing, Gussy swayed slightly back and forth, a vacant look on her face.

Jed tapped her on the shoulder, a buddy-buddy gesture if she'd ever felt one. "Thanks for dessert," he said with a jolly camaraderie, and disappeared into the night.

Eventually Gussy teetered two steps over and slumped down onto the pink granite rim of the fountain. The thorny brambles that clung to its base snagged her hose and scratched her legs. She didn't notice. She was trying to wrap her mind around the gargantuan difference between the way that Jed had kissed her and the way that he had treated her afterward.

For her, the earth had moved. For him, apparently, the earth had continued on as before without even a wobble.

Goodness gracious. Was this how Andrews had felt when they'd gone all the way on the deck of his sailboat the night of Gussy's sixteenth birthday because April was leaving for college in a week and Gussy had been afraid that the world was passing her by? When afterward she'd barely managed to withhold her disappointment and the tears that had sprung to her eyes, and then the next day told Andrews she thought they should be only friends?

If so, poor Andrews.

Poor Gussy.

ON THE MORNING of the second day of the rest of her life, Gussy was not so giddily optimistic. She'd spent ten minutes with Great-grandfather, listening to him complain about the drafts that whistled beneath his door and the wind that rattled the windowpanes despite closed shutters and drapes of wool-lined velvet. That was followed by breakfast with Grandmother, who was in an unusually querulous mood and had fretted endlessly over what to do with April's butler. Godfrey, apparently not one to wait for directions, had already taken over the kitchen. In his usual insidious, butler-type way, Thwaite had let it be known that he was not a happy camper, but Gussy thought the French toast was delicious.

"Put on your gum boots, Augustina," Marian said as she directed the reluctant Gussy toward the mud room. They were to meet Jed in the front garden at 8:00 a.m. and Marian was never late. "Where's your sweater, child? The weather's nippy."

"I am not a five-year-old, Grandmother. And besides, it's plenty warm outside. It's almost the end of July, for pity's sake."

"I don't know what's wrong with you lately." Marian wore an ancient balmacaan draped around her shoulders like a cape and beneath it, a wool crepe suit and a Barbara Bush three-strand pearl choker. "You're as nervous as a cat."

Gussy shoved her feet into the boots without answering. "I'm going to let Percy out," she said shortly, and escaped to the outdoors. Sending pebbles scattering in her wake, she ran through the parking court and then across the lawn to the kennel with her hair streaming loose, her fierce expression an echo of the times in her childhood when the estate's woods, meadows and shoreline had seemed her only refuge. April had preferred curling up with a book of fairy tales or an old black-and-white movie on TV, but staying indoors had stifled Gussy to distraction. All she'd ever craved was to be as free as the wind.

However, today she was escaping a more adult dilemma—the memory of Jed's casual dismissal of their kiss. A kiss that had meant everything to Gussy at the time, but was now just another humiliating moment in the exceedingly humiliating saga of her life. All she could hope was that Jed had no inkling of her feelings and she would be spared *that* embarrassment when they met up again five minutes from now.

Percy, bless him, greeted her ecstatically. There was a good reason people became so attached to their dogs, Gussy decided, gratefully hugging the retriever's furry golden body. Percy squirmed free and nosed past the kennel door to bound across the damp lawn, barking at the gulls that rose, flapping and screeching, from the craggy cliffside.

Gussy gave herself a minute to compose herself as she studied the monochromatic sky and water. Although it was a damp gray morning, the sun, presently a flat disk paled by the mist, was doing its best to make an appearance.

She decided that she'd be friendly but remote, relaxed yet no-nonsense. Jed would see that their kiss meant as little to her as it did to him. If he should ever happen to mention it, she'd toss her head and laugh like Vanessa Van Pelt. Why, Jed, she'd say, did you kiss me? Why, Jed, I'm kissed so often, I couldn't possibly recall yours specifically!

Percy raced toward the house. Moments later, Gussy, still staring out to the sea, heard Marian's disgruntled exclamations. "Down, Percy, down! Augustina! Augustina!"

Time to face the music.

Resigned, she trudged back up the slope to the front garden. Her grandmother was pointing at the herbaceous border and pontificating on how she wanted it maintained. Jed was kneeling beside Percy, letting the dog lick his hand while he, by all appearances, watched for Gussy. She hesitated, then came around the corner of the house with her head hung low and her fists shoved deep into the pockets of her baggy chinos, but looked up defiantly when Jed rose. "Good morning, Mr. Kelley," she said, squeezing the words out of her tight throat.

His eyebrows went up a notch. He nodded. "Good morning to you, Miss Fairchild."

"Shall we tour the garden?"

"Lead on."

Gussy's lips pursed. This wasn't going the way it should. She hadn't meant to come off like a prissy, rejected virgin. She wanted Jed to be confused, not amused. But what could she do—exclaim that she didn't care one whit that he hadn't enjoyed kissing her as much as she'd adored kissing him? In front of Grandmother?

Marian stepped to the front, tapping her umbrella on the stone steps. "Come along. We'll look at the rose garden first. Do you know your roses, Mr. Kelley?"

"It's not my strongest point, I'll admit. Jellicoe didn't use many roses."

"Jellicoe?" Gussy repeated with surprise. "Broadnax Jellicoe, the British gardening legend? You worked with him?"

"*For* him," Jed said. "Nobody works 'with' Jellicoe."

"I believe I gave you Mr. Kelley's résumé, Augustina."

"Uh, yes, Grandmother, you did." Gussy couldn't remember reading it, though; she'd been too shell-shocked by other developments. She shot Jed a suspicious look. "I thought you were a hockey player."

"From ages sixteen to twenty-two, I spent every summer as Jellicoe's lowliest horticultural apprentice, after he'd moved to New England to set American gardening to rights. He was a little peeved when I gave it up for professional hockey. I think his last words to me were *you'll never plant another pine or pot another petunia.*"

"Oh, dear," said Gussy. "Does he hold a grudge?"

Even Marian looked a tad worried. Jellicoe's legendary reputation as a horticultural dictator was firmly intact even though he'd been retired for several years. If he'd laid down the law, Jed Kelley would be persona non grata to the society of gardeners for miles around. He'd have to be fired.

Jed seemed unconcerned. "Not to worry. He always growled the most at the favored workers. It was the only way an apprentice knew he'd been noticed."

They'd come to the rose garden, softly glowing in shades of rose, cream and lemon in the limpid morning light. The jeweled greens of the foliage glimmered with dew. A pristine white lattice gazebo overlooked the ocean, where the brisk wind blew away the last of the lingering fog. The sun winked brighter in between banks of scudding clouds.

They entered the garden through a wide arched arbor thickly cloaked with pink roses. "New Dawn," Marian said, pointing with the tip of her umbrella as she led the way. "And the apricot ones are Queen Margot. Very fussy."

Gussy hesitated beneath the shadowed archway. It was

the perfect location for a sweet, stolen kiss, but when Jed came up from behind and touched her shoulder she darted through to the other side, her boots skidding on the stone path. Marching around the hexagonal layout of the rose garden, listening with one ear to her grandmother's favorite recipe for aphid baths, Gussy decided that she must rid herself of such romantic notions as stolen kisses if she was to marry for freedom and not love. Although it had been an easier task before Jed's appearance on the scene, imagining herself as the very proper and very dull Mrs. Andrews Lowell ought to do it.

Jed was being very quiet. Gussy wasn't sure if that was because of last night's somewhat truncated kiss or if it was his usual method of operation. Obviously Grandmother liked the unquestioning quality of it; Gussy sensed that in Jed's case silence did not necessarily mean compliance, as it often did with herself. He would do as he wanted without a lot of discussion or confrontation—something for her to consider. Maybe she didn't *have* to become Mrs. Andrews Lowell....

"Black spot," Jed said suddenly.

"What?" Marian was insulted at the mere possibility.

Gently Jed twisted one of the canes to show them the spots growing on its inner leaves. Gussy bent to look closer, her attention caught by the sure but careful movements of Jed's hands rather than fungus problems. Without speaking, he took her hand and brushed her fingertips over the fuzzy leaves, then thankfully released it before the arousal that was rolling through her body could erupt in potentially embarrassing ways.

"He's right," she said to her grandmother, her voice cracking. *He's absolutely right,* echoed her heart. "Oh, dear," she sighed, mostly to herself.

"Why, I never." Marian hung the handle of the umbrella on her wrist and peered through her half-moon reading glasses. "Black spot! In the Throckmorton rose garden!"

"I can take care of it with a simple spray. Nothing to it."

"It seems I hired you just in the nick of time, Mr. Kelley." Marian snapped the glasses back into their needlepoint case. "Let me show you the rhododendron allée. It's getting rather ragged. And we should inspect the hydrangeas that are threatening to overtake the terrace wall."

Jed's glance slid to Gussy. Today his eyes were the soothing blue of a calm ocean, lapping her with a look that was as gentle as his hands. She smiled bravely, despite her quaking resolutions. So much for Andrews and their convenient marriage.

So much for detachment.

Gussy knew that wanting Jed, choosing Jed, would put her in a worse quagmire than before. One that would take more than gum boots to get out of.

5

Sweet Poison

"VERY CAPABILITY BROWN," Jed said, overlooking the vista of the parkway with its smooth, rolling turf and majestic, encircling woodland.

Gussy recognized the name of another renowned English landscape designer, before even Jellicoe's time. "You know your stuff."

"I get the feeling you thought there were other reasons your grandmother hired me."

Remembering, Gussy blushed. "I told you—it was only a temporary mix-up."

Marian was striding along the allée, flapping her balmacaan at Percy to shoo him out of the rows of tall, decades-old rhododendrons. Every time she succeeded in chasing the dog from one end, he crashed through elsewhere in a confetti of leaves, barking with exuberance, oblivious to Marian's ire. Gussy knew she should go and retrieve Percy before he did too much damage, but she wanted only to stand in the sunshine and smile at Jed.

She'd forgotten that she was going to be cool toward him. She'd forgotten that he wasn't appropriate for the Throckmorton heiress's husband. She'd definitely forgotten to call herself Mrs. Andrews Lowell.

Marian gave up. "Augustina, please lock Percy in the kennel." She brushed at her suit, straightening the braided trim. "I must leave for my luncheon appointment. I can see no reason why I shouldn't put Godfrey to good use by employing him as my driver." After folding her coat over her arm, she marched up the gravel path to the house, using the folded umbrella like a cane, saying over her shoulder, "And why don't you accompany Mr. Kelley to the Sheepshead Bay Nursery to introduce him around, Augustina? I don't want old Padgett thinking he can palm off second-rate conifers on our new gardener."

"Yes, ma'am," Gussy replied obediently, her mind immediately reeling with thoughts of being alone with Jed for at least an hour. Maybe two. The steam heat that had collected inside her rubber boots transferred itself to her face. She turned as pink as a boiled shrimp.

Jed also agreed readily. "I'll get my pickup and meet you at the front door."

Was Gussy imagining it or did he looked pleased at the prospect? "I—I...okay," she mumbled.

After a moment of silence, Jed said, "About that kiss..."

She tried to laugh with gay abandon and wound up sounding more like one of the squawking gulls. "Why, Jed, it was nothing!" she insisted. "A mere trifle! A momentary whim!" Her hands fluttered frantically; she was too nervous to notice Jed's clouding expression. "I've already forgotten it!"

"Then so will I," he vowed.

"A silly impulse! A lapse in—"

"You have five minutes, Miss Fairchild."

"—good judgment," Gussy finished in a whisper, watching the hard-as-granite cut of Jed's shoulders as he walked away.

She doubted that Vanessa Van Pelt ever felt such regret.

THE QUAYSIDE SPARKLED with color and activity. Jed and Gussy sat at one of the Bobber & Buoy Inn's outdoor tables, on a weathered wood deck built over a jumble of boulders whose mollusk-speckled skirts of wet green moss were temporarily revealed by the outgoing tide. The marine smell of kelp and salt thickened the dazzling sunlit air.

Gussy felt easier in her skin. They'd spent an hour at the local greenhouse, talking stiffly at first and then finally more comfortably about the Throckmorton Cottage plantings and what Jed needed to replace before fall. Jed had spoken straight but respectfully to Tink Padgett, the crafty owner who didn't suffer dumb greenhorns gladly, and had come away with a truck bed full of trees and shrubs at a very good price.

Gussy's presence had been superfluous. Riding back through town in Jed's red pickup, she'd even started to wonder if he was suffering *her,* maybe not so gladly, either, on the say-so of her grandmother. Certainly he didn't seem to need her college-botany-degree advice.

Still, if he was suffering, he didn't show it. She'd try to do the same, even though what she was suffering was her own misgivings. The need to continue her quest for independence without betraying her suddenly resoundingly romantic heart had her all twisted up into knots inside, knots as tight, swollen and encrusted as the sailor's hitches hung in loops on the board-and-batten walls of the saltbox inn. Gussy had to smile to herself at the predictable motif; if she was in a cage, it must be a lobster trap. They were also employed as decor, painted vivid turquoise and orange by the inn's transplanted city-folk owners, dangling from the deck railing in between flower boxes bursting with geraniums, lobelia, petunias and pinks.

Jed had relaxed back in his chair, his face turned toward

the harbor as he watched a sloop set sail. The cuffs of his chambray work shirt were turned up over his forearms, where short dark hair curled against his tan skin.

Gussy dipped her head to reach the plastic straw of her soft drink. "Your glasses look just like mine."

"I forgot I had them on." He plucked off the wire-frame glasses and casually tossed them onto the silvery wood tabletop.

Gussy reached out, drew back her hand, then when Jed looked again at the sailboat, furtively let one fingertip slide along the gold wire earpiece. It was warm from his skin; her toes flexed beneath the leather straps of her sandals. Again she withdrew, taking up her cup and stirring the straw, stabbing at the ice. She was acting entirely too besotted!

Jed rubbed the bridge of his nose. "I wear them mostly for driving. Remember Howitzer O'Hallihan?" He tapped his scar. "Howitzer also temporarily detached my retina when he split open my temple. Once in a while I still have a bout with blurred vision."

"Did the league put Howitzer in jail?"

"Hell, no." Jed laughed. "He probably got a trophy for making the Hit of the Week."

"But that's terrible!"

"That's hockey."

Gussy squinched her nose. "I'm not much of a hockey fan, so as far as I know you're a major superstar with billion-dollar endorsement deals, Jed Kelley trading cards and what all. Should I be awestruck to be having lunch with you? Should I get your autograph?"

He made a dismissive snort. "I'm just a regular guy."

Hardly that. She smiled to herself. *And hockey has nothing to do with it.*

"How did you land a summer job with Jellicoe?" she

asked. "I've heard that he turns away droves of applicants, even now that he's retired."

"Connections. He was consulting with the group that was overseeing the restoration of an historic estate garden in Massachusetts. My mother was the chairperson. He liked her because he couldn't intimidate her."

Gussy was eager for gossip. "Did Jellicoe really snub both Princess Grace and Babe Paley? And is it true that he only hires men?"

Jed shrugged. "He snubs everyone."

"And?"

He leaned back even farther, playfully tipping the chair out of her reach. "Don't take off my head, but, yes, it's true. He won't employ women. Says they're amateurs, should only putter in their own backyards." He held up his hands, palms out. "Not that I agree."

"If you worked for him, you agreed by silent assent." She made a face. "But I'm not a good person to protest. I haven't done a thing with my own degree, professionally speaking, so I guess…"

Jed tipped forward and the chair legs hit the deck with a thud. "Why not?"

"There's a good question." Gussy tried to think why she'd fallen into her plush but unproductive way of life. Probably because it was easiest to do what everyone had expected of her—which was essentially nothing serious, only maintaining the appropriate social calendar and volunteering where needed.

She attempted another carefree laugh; maybe she'd get better at it with practice. "The world needs a healthy supply of strictly decorative heiresses, don't you think?"

Jed was noncommittal. "I guess it takes all kinds."

"You really want to say 'Get a job,' but you can't because you're my job, more or less."

"Probably less."

Her eyes narrowed. "What does that mean?"

He shrugged.

"I hate men who've graduated from the Gary Cooper School of Laconic Communication."

Jed's grin flashed unexpectedly. Every time it did, his eyes glinted like sapphires under a spotlight, which was very challenging to her sense of decorum.

"Men are physical," he said. "Women are verbal. Men kind of like it that way because—"

"Do you mean oral?" she asked, surrendering to the kind of mischievous impulse she hadn't known she possessed—up to now.

He cocked his head. This time his eyes didn't glint; they glittered, provoking Gussy far beyond good behavior. She elaborated. "Men like it when women are *oral,* not so much verbal—"

Jed interrupted. "Are you forgetting that I'm your gardener? Not one of the cast of thousands you call boyfriends?"

"Thousands? I don't—"

"Okay, then, dozens, wasn't it?" He shifted uneasily, glancing around the deck as if he was desperate for their waitress—or anyone else—to interrupt.

Gussy wasn't sure what had happened, but she knew she'd been jolted from her rock-steady path of boredom and propriety. She felt stimulated, witty, alive. She even felt alluring. Suggestive repartee wasn't her custom, but since he was reacting to her as a woman and not a mouse...

"Care to make it a baker's dozen?" she teased.

With no timely distractions to be had, Jed reluctantly turned to face her. His stare was level and lengthy before he finally found the wherewithal to respond negatively to what had surely been a frivolous invitation. "Not on a bet," he said.

He felt as slimy as seaweed when Gussy's face crumpled. "Oh," she whispered, turning a lovely mottled pink. "Sorry."

He tried to make amends. "Don't take offense. See, I have this aversion to crowds. I tend to get lost in them."

She still looked miserable, and why was that when by all accounts she already had more suitors than she needed? Jed couldn't figure it out. One instant Gussy was flighty and flirtatious, the next vulnerable and shy. Last night she'd been ready to pollinate, then by morning she was as brittle as a corn husk in November. It *was* enough to make a man laconic—he didn't dare open his mouth because he was sure to say the wrong thing to the wrong Gussy.

Then again, it could be his own feelings that were confused. He had to admit that despite his avowal not to let it happen, he was more and more drawn to Miss Augustina Fairchild. On the surface she was the self-described decorative heiress without a serious concern, but below that…well, there was much about her outlook and tastes that seemed to mesh with his own. And when she forgot herself, she was sweet and delightful and fascinating and funny. Any woman who could recite the characteristics of sixteen varieties of irises wasn't entirely useless.

Finally the waitress arrived, bringing a basket of warm, nutty bread, Gussy's Caesar salad and Jed's clam chowder. Gussy kept her face turned down, concentrating on her lunch, although Jed soon noticed that she was pushing forkfuls of it around her plate instead of eating.

"It's not a good idea to mix business with pleasure," he said cautiously. "I shouldn't have kissed—"

"Why, Jed! Why, Jed, I…" Her voice started out bright and hard, but faded fast. She shook her head and mumbled,

"You're right." Two beats later, she looked up accusingly. "What about Vanessa Van Pelt?"

"What about her?"

Gussy waved her fork in a little circle. "Don't tell me Vanessa hasn't tried...you know."

"Tried, but not succeeded."

Gussy tipped up her chin. "Yes, I can see it. Women throwing themselves at you left and right, yet Jed Kelley remains a paragon of virtue."

At least she was no longer looking so dejected. "I never said I *never* said yes," he admitted.

"But not to a client?"

"Definitely not." In the case of the amorous heiress, that wasn't easy. And he could foresee it getting even tougher.

Although Gussy was pretending to watch the harbor, her brown-penny gaze kept sliding sideways with little flicks and flutters of her lashes. Her open, expressive face prompted an undefined ache inside Jed.

Her brow furrowed as if she was deep in thought. Her lips parted without a sound, then, eventually, came a tentative speculation, spoken with a soft, lazy, sun-drenched hum that oozed through him, sharpening his need. "What if I wasn't a client?"

Though he had no idea what she had in mind, the possibilities made his world tilt on its axis.

"MACHINE GUN KELLEY!"

Jed blinked.

"Jed, is that you?" boomed the disruptive voice, busting into itty-bitty pieces the very nice fantasy that Jed had instantly conjured at Gussy's soft insinuation. "Hot damn! Whaddya know—Machine Gun Kelley!"

Gussy chortled. "Machine Gun?"

Jed groaned. "I'd say 'Don't ask,' but I think you're about to find out."

A bear of a man with a gap-toothed grin jogged up the deck steps from the direction of the wharf. He was as burly and blunt-featured as a longshoreman, although he wore madras shorts, a Maine Berrypickers Union T-shirt and neon green flip-flops. His accent was heavily Canadian. "Well, well, Jed! It's a small world, isn't it?"

Jed stood and shook hands. "Bronson," he said with a smile. "Good to see you."

"Who's the girlfriend?" Bronson asked immediately. "Glad to see that you're not brooding over Julie."

Jed saw the flash of copper in Gussy's eyes, then the slow speculation as she carefully smoothed her expression. "Gussy, this is Steve Bronson, my former teammate."

"Been retired three years now," Bronson said.

"Bronson, Gussy Fairchild. A local girl." Jed purposely used a description bland enough to divert attention. He didn't want to get into some drawn-out discussion of how he'd found Julie's replacement. "What brings you to Maine, Bronson?"

"I needed the vacation after visiting Sue's parents in Nova Scotia. We're waiting for the ferry—that's Sue Anne and little Bronnie feeding the gulls." Bronson waved at the wife and son, who were standing at the end of the wharf tossing hunks of bread to the gulls swooping and spiraling around them. "Come September, I'm back in Ottawa teaching squirts how to bodycheck. Looks like you've got it better than me." He thrust a robust elbow at Jed's flat midriff.

"Oof," Jed said.

Bronson thought that was hilarious. "Yup, yah shot the puck like a machine gun, but yah never could take the blindside check!"

"Thank God I no longer have to," Jed said. "Running a gardening business is easier on the body."

Bronson was eyeing Gussy as if she were a piece of pie à la mode. "Yum-yum," he said with crude admiration.

"The gardens of Gussy's family estate are my biggest—"

Bronson just laughed. "Hey, man, what do you need with Julie—let Pierre have her."

Jed felt his expression freeze. "So she's with Pierre now? Why am I not surprised?"

Bronson waved his arms. "Forget her!"

Jed tensed, waiting for Gussy to ask. She smiled sweetly at his former teammate instead. "Are you taking the ferry to Osprey Island? Don't miss the view from the northeastern point." She chatted about the island's cranberry bog and the protected habitat of the ospreys until the ferry blatted its horn and Bronson left them at a gallop, waving and shouting his goodbyes.

Now she'll ask, Jed thought.

She didn't. She buttered a piece of bread.

Jed ate a spoonful of his chowder. Then another. Gussy picked up her drink and smiled pleasantly at him over the rim.

"Julie Cole was my fiancée," he blurted, then almost bit his tongue. Why had he felt the need to confess *that?* The entire regrettable affair was best forgotten—not that he could. Its effects still lingered.

Gussy looked alert but heedful. "What happened?"

"Howitzer O'Hallihan."

"Howitzer, Machine Gun…hockey must be a very violent sport."

"Indoor sports can be just as dangerous."

"Are you referring to Julie?" Gussy cocked her head;

sunshine flashed on her glasses. "But Julie is such a sweet name."

Jed measured his reply. "Sometimes the sweetness only temporarily disguises the bitter aftertaste."

"Oh, dear," Gussy murmured. "She done you wrong."

He couldn't eat any more of the chowder. He couldn't take any more of Gussy's circumspect responses, either. "You're the most confounding, contrary woman I ever met," he complained. "Aren't you even curious?"

She acted surprised. "I thought you'd be impressed by my restraint. After all, we wouldn't want to confuse our business relationship with personal references."

"Touché."

She relented, her eyes gone soft and velvety. "So tell me what happened after Howitzer happened."

"I found out that Julie liked me more as a star hockey player making big bucks than as an injured ex-hockey player needing a new career. Looking back, it shouldn't have come as such a surprise."

"Who broke up with whom?"

"By the time she actually returned the ring, it was mutual. It's kind of hard for a guy to stay engaged when his fiancée is already scouting among the Whalers' roster for a replacement."

"So then this Pierre guy is a hockey player?"

"Julie upgraded. Pierre *does* have endorsement deals and trading cards and fan clubs. But if he wants Julie to stick around, he'd better not lose them. She likes status."

Gussy looked at him sorrowfully.

Damn. Jed put his head in his hands, swearing to himself, wishing he'd kept the whole sorry saga under wraps. He didn't need to have the amorous heiress thinking of ways to buck up his self-esteem. It was doing fine, thank you. He'd learned a hard lesson, suffered a little, but now he had his head on straight and his life focused. Never again would he be susceptible to one whose sweet girlish charm was not entirely natural, but practiced.

Like Gussy, he thought. *Maybe.*

He should proceed with the utmost caution. In hockey, he'd learned how dangerous it was to turn your back on someone with the power to blast you out of your skates.

He was afraid that Gussy was gaining that power. He wasn't sure that she knew it, though. Unless she was a very good actress.

He looked up, smoothing one hand across his shorn skull. Gussy's eyes were big and round, glistening like chocolate melting in the sun. "Andrews made a crack," she said, "about gardening being a comedown after pro hockey. Do you feel that way? Do you miss all the glamour and prestige?"

"Not that." He drained his iced tea before continuing. "I miss the game, yeah. Having to quit so abruptly was tough to handle. But by the time I'd rehabbed my knee I was past that. Since I'd always liked gardening, and I wanted to stay busy..." He shrugged. "Here I am."

"Well, I'm glad you ended up in Sheepshead Bay," she said softly.

Despite his misgivings, Jed smiled. He looked at the billowing cumulus clouds, the briny water lapping at the gray stone and weathered pillars of the quay and the stark beauty of the evergreens etched against the cobalt sky. He looked at Gussy, her chin propped on her hands, her baggy pant legs flapping in the wind and her face, her solemn eyes, her rosy lips so soft and sweet, so sweet....

"So am I," he agreed.

6

The Amorous Heiress and Co.

IT WAS A BUSY WEEK. It was also a very long week.

At least for Jed. He suspected Gussy was of another opinion—she'd certainly *seemed* to be enjoying herself.

Tuesday, he'd been demonstrating the proper way to clip boxwood to one of his part-time workers when Andrews Lowell arrived to take Gussy out to lunch. Jed happened to be kneeling out of sight behind one of the topiary bushes when they emerged from the house, laughing and chatting and looking very *Town & Country*. "Where did Jed go?" Gussy asked, but at that point he wasn't about to pop up in his overalls and grovel for her attention. Andrews had hustled her along with promises of lobster bisque and no Felicity and Ted.

Thursday, Marian Throckmorton called for Jed to bring the Rolls-Royce up to the parking court because she was on her way to tea at the Gilmores'. He obeyed, secretly hoping for a glimpse of Gussy. She obliged, coming out the side door right behind her grandmother, frowning as she tugged at a pair of white gloves. Jed held the car door open in temporary-chauffeur fashion. Gussy watched him from beneath the brim of a pert straw hat until he winked devilishly at her to see how she'd respond. She turned away, flustered, her cheeks pinkening, her high heels mincing on the gravel as she scooted around to the other side of the car and got in. They didn't exchange a word.

Friday was hot, and Jed was late coming home from overseeing the resodding of the Van Pelts' lawn. He'd just parked at the carriage house, stepped out and stripped off his sweaty T-shirt when Gussy zipped past in the passenger side of some playboy's seventy-five-thousand-dollar onyx Raptor convertible. He caught only a glimpse of her face—eyes wide open, mouth even wider, one hand clamped to her hairdo and the other scrambling for the seat belt. Jed wadded up his shirt, tossed it in the back of the pickup and without stopping to think about what he was doing crossed the estate grounds and climbed down the steep stone stairway to the beach in record time, his mind fuming and his body made acutely painful by thoughts of the amorous heiress and her equally amorous suitors. As the sun set in an orange-red-violet splendor, he dunked himself again and again in the freezing ocean and asked a higher power to grant him the strength to withstand the sweet poison of Gussy's allure. Innocent or not, she was an imminent danger to his vital parts.

When Saturday finally arrived, Jed made himself work until noon on a new client's perennial garden even though on the way through town all the traffic was going in the opposite direction. The air was giddy with the holiday feeling of the regatta, but it was Gussy's image that burned in his mind while he staked delphiniums and watered the languishing phlox. She would be smiling, looking deceptively shy and old-fashioned as she passed out lemonade to an endless parade of her admirers.

Finally Jed gave up, washed himself with the hose, collected his gardening tools and headed back toward town. Gussy had personally issued him an invitation to her refreshment booth. She was probably looking for him.

Sheepshead Bay was bursting with tourists. People in two-hundred-dollar sunglasses and trendy beachwear mobbed the town, exclaiming over the quaint shingled fishing shacks and Cape Cod–style cottages and the charming crooked streets, buying up every blueberry pie and authentically weathered weather vane in sight. Most of the activity was centered at the booths ringing the harbor, where pure white and rainbow-striped sails danced across the water. The scent of buttery popcorn and corn on the cob, sizzling deep-fried fish and seaweed mingled among the shouts, laughter, tinny music and occasional booming announcement over the loudspeakers. A starting gun popped and a cheer went up, onshore and off.

Jed bought a whitefish sandwich. Chewing, he bypassed the cloying perfume of the flower-show tent, where Marian Throckmorton presided over a dozen babbling ladies as colorful in their print silk dresses as the triple-tier aisles of fussy floral arrangements.

The garden club's refreshment booth was decorated with a fringe of freshly cut fir boughs; a sharp, resinous tang hung in the air. Wet glass pitchers of lemonade sat in a row, tempting potential customers. Miss Augustina Fairchild, in white cotton with a pale yellow sweater tied around her shoulders, was even more tempting to at least one of them.

Jed licked his lips.

He thought her eyes lit up when she saw him. "Lemonade?" she asked, slightly out of breath.

He looked at the iced lemonade decorated with sprigs of mint, then back up at Gussy's open, glowing face. She couldn't be that guileless and a vamp, too. Could she? He laid a twenty-dollar bill on the table. "I'll take a pitcher."

"A pitcher?"

"I told you I'd be thirsty."

Clucking her tongue, she shook her head so her long, thick brown braid swung from shoulder to shoulder. The ice cubes clattered when she poured. "I'll start you with a glass."

He finished it in one long swig and handed it back. Smiling, she poured him another. "Have you done your duty for the garden club?" he asked, thumbing up the droplets that had trickled from the sweating glass and down the side of his mouth.

Coyly, Gussy peeped at him from the corner of her eye. "What did you have in mind?"

"First off, getting you out of here before Andrews shows up."

She laughed appreciatively. "Sally, would you take over the counter for me?"

A girl with a round, freckled face looked Jed up and down. "*Shu-ure* thing."

Gussy slung a tiny needlepoint purse with an extra-long strap across her torso, leaving her hands free. Jed drained his second ten-dollar glass of lemonade without regret at the cost and took one of her hands before it was no longer free. "What *did* you have in mind?" she asked.

"You might slap my face if I told you."

Her eyes widened. "Is that why you're holding on so tight?"

Her hand was soft, warm, delicate. He wanted to rub it across his chest, wanted to taste it with his lips, wanted to feel it moving down his body. "One of the reasons."

Gussy was enthralled by the contact, but wary. She could feel the stares beaming at the back of her head, could maybe even hear the hiss and spit of percolating gossip. Holding hands with the gardener was definitely not done in the Throckmorton's circle—at least not publicly. But then, had Gussy ever consciously chosen to become a part of the circle? Her inclusion was an accident of blue-blooded birth. If she had any gumption, she would do as she liked and let the stuffy prigs sputter all they wanted.

"As long as they're good reasons," she said, planting an overly enthusiastic kiss on Jed's jaw. That would show them!

He glanced down, the color of his irises deepening. "Maybe bad is better."

She giggled; he brought out of her a long-buried bent for flirtation. "Why, Jed, you're not bad, you're wicked!" she bantered, but her voice was a touch too shrill. She couldn't quite maintain the proper level.

He gave her a raised-eyebrow look of caution. "Where's the best place to watch the regatta?"

"From either the porch of the yacht club or the deck of Felicity and Ted's new house on the point." She nodded toward an ostentatiously modern structure jutting out over the fingertip of the rocky peninsula that formed one side of the bay. "We'll run into my grandmother at the former and Andrews at the latter."

"Better to avoid both, I'd say."

She was glad he saw the wisdom in that. "There is another place I know of, out on the rocks, a little tricky to reach, but..."

"But what?"

She looked sheepish. "It's best known as a make-out place to the local teenagers. At least once evening comes."

"Sounds good."

Her eyebrows went up.

"The view, I mean," he said. "Not the other."

"Of course not," she agreed, admirably holding a wave of disappointment at bay. A boisterous family surged around them, holding sticks of pink cotton candy. "We're too adult for that sort of thing," she continued once the family had passed, her stare centered on the vivid, jumbled patterns of the Episcopal Sisterhood's quilt display. "I imagine it's awfully cold and hard and uncomfortable out on those rocks at night."

"Don't you know firsthand?" Jed asked lightly, squinting at the sailboats rounding a buoy.

She couldn't help but grin at the far-fetched likelihood of a local boy having asked April's quiet, plain, younger sister to join him at Make-out Rocks.

Jed picked up on her small smile; it seemed knowing to him. "I guess you'd better not answer that question unless you want to incriminate yourself." He started off without waiting for an answer, taking up her hand to tug her along. "Let's go."

Gussy scrambled after him. "Wrong way!" She steered him back around. They held hands all the way past the eagle-eyed church ladies and even the open entrance of the canvas flower tent, neither of them daring to look inside should Marian Throckmorton be looking out. Leaving the main crowd, they turned down a bricked alley behind the fish market. They crossed a short, narrow causeway, slippery with lichen and sea foam, and then came to the rocks, jagged peaks on one side, flattened out to several levels of smooth plateaus on the other. Below, a group of teenagers had staked out a pebbly patch of the shingle beach.

"This way," Gussy said. On the seat of her white duck trousers she slid down dark rocks worn smooth by the surf, leading him to a nook where they'd be sheltered from the wind yet still have a grand view of the harbor. Sleek, graceful sloops were gathering for the last race of the afternoon, skimming the water like osprey on the hunt.

"Beautiful," Jed said. He was looking at Gussy.

"Mmm, yes," she agreed. "I used to come here all the time. When the tide was out I'd climb down to find the tidal pools hidden among the rocks, tiny jewels, worlds unto themselves, and farther along by the steep cliffs there's a marvelous cave with anemones growing in the dark…so quiet and mysterious and scary, but beautiful. Really beautiful.''

She didn't sound like a femme fatale. Didn't look like one, either. Wisps of her hair had worked free from the braid and were flying about her face. Her cheeks were ruddy, her eyes, undisguised for once by the lenses and frames of her missing glasses, were filled with a crystal, amber light. Jed was infused with a longing that was more than physical. It defied all his other instincts. He stayed silent for several heartbeats, listening to the hiss of the waves and the clang of the buoy. Listening to his inner voice.

They spoke at once. ''Where's your glasses—''

''So how's business—''

She smiled. ''I'm wearing contacts. I do sometimes.''

He smiled. ''Business is picking up. But I'll be doing a lot of the manual labor myself until I'm busy enough to hire full-time help.''

''Maybe you should give me a job,'' she suggested lightly. ''I'm honest and dependable. And I don't need a high wage. That's one benefit of living with my grandparents, anyway.''

Pragmatic reasons for restraint began to seep back into Jed's reasoning. He desperately wanted to believe that being sensible was a good thing and surrendering to his senses was not. ''Have you ever in your life held down a job for any length of time?''

Gussy dropped her chin onto her bent knees, watching her fingertip trace patterns on the smooth ledge beneath them. ''I had a college internship at Collingswood Gardens. And I've done a lot of gardening work—volunteer—

for various groups since then. I organized the group who landscaped Sheepshead Bay's town park.'' She frowned, rubbing at a bit of white quartz embedded in the black rock. "It doesn't sound like much, does it?"

Jed didn't want her to feel worthless. From an heiress's point of view, she had no reason to. Why should she work for a wage she didn't need? "That sort of thing is a vital contribution, Gussy. It really is."

"Still, it's not the same as earning a paycheck."

"Well...I think it's possible you might gain some independence if you did decide to find a job. That's all."

She looked at him questioningly.

He patted her shoulder. "Sorry. I'm not hiring at the moment."

Her sudden laugh was staccato. She sat up straighter, tossing her braid over her shoulder, shrugging off his comment. "No need for apology. It's not like I was serious! Why, I'm so busy already, with my needlepoint projects and my family obligations and my—"

"Social schedule," Jed interjected.

"Oh, yes, absolutely! My calendar is stuffed to the gills with dates for sailing and golfing and dinners and dances...."

"Yeah, I got that idea."

"I'll probably be getting engaged any day now."

Jed's heart shrank. "Is that so?" he said, laconic to the death.

She nodded energetically. "Oh, yes, absolutely."

"Who's the lucky guy? Andrews?"

"Maybe. Or maybe it'll be Billy or Peter Gilmore."

"Or the playboy bachelor in the black Raptor who doesn't care if he runs you up a tree."

"Edward Peasport III," she supplied solemnly, making

Jed laugh. It was a harsh sound; she offered a weak smile in response. "I don't think it'll be Edward Peasport III."

"At least you have the sense to eliminate *someone*." Besides himself, he added silently, although he wasn't entirely sure that she had—as far as extracurriculars went.

Gussy was remembering the harried ride with Edward and her fleeting sighting of Jed, shirtless and gleaming with perspiration, so potently male that the yearning of her feminine impulses had been almost painful. That she would react so strongly to only a glimpse of Jed had effectively ruined any chance Edward had with her—even if he hadn't turned out to be as thick as his billfold.

She sighed, knowing she'd lied to Jed. She was further from becoming engaged and independent than ever. And the reason was sitting beside her.

Jed Kelley.

Gussy tried to watch the regatta even though all her thoughts were concentrated on Jed. He was primal, earthy, intense, unlike any man she'd ever known. They'd each attempted to deflect their growing attraction—Jed by putting her off after she'd kissed him and he'd returned the kiss a hundredfold; Gussy by pretending that she was seriously interested in Andrews and the others. She knew it hadn't worked for her part, and she suspected it hadn't blunted Jed's feelings, either. Though she was mainly inexperienced except for the one time with Andrews and a few humdrum relationships with college guys, being the subject of one of Jed's vital electric blue looks would make even the most naive of girls aware of his intent.

His intent was part of her problem. She was too meek and mousy for a wildly inappropriate affair. Frankly, if she were capable of that, she'd be capable of *anything*.

Maybe that was what scared her. Letting go, breaking

free, giving up all Throckmorton-supplied safety, security and convenience.

Truly being her own woman. Truly taking charge of her life.

No. Gussy shuddered with the realization. She couldn't do it. She was too much a coward.

Jed put his arm around her. "Cold?"

"Umm," she murmured, purposely noncommittal as she leaned into him, letting herself rely on his ready strength. Dangerous, that. But momentarily okay.

Very okay. Jed smelled like the earth, rich with sunshine and rainwater and the salty wind off the ocean. An addictive scent. She looked up at his face, examining the hollow cheeks, the white line of the scar, the broken bones mended stronger than ever. He was hardened. He was a survivor.

Emotionally, too? Gussy thought of Julie Cole, picturing Jed loving another woman, asking her to marry him. Her heart ached with jealousy and possessiveness—things she had no right to feel.

Yet emotion had no logic. She lifted her head and nuzzled his neck. His skin was damp from the fine mist that hung in the air; her tongue took a slow, savoring lick of the underside of his jaw before guiltily withdrawing. Why was the impulse to touch and taste and stroke this one man so persistent that at every turn her usual reticence was overwhelmed?

Jed shifted against the rock ledge, taking Gussy fully into his arms. She raised one hand, wanting to caress his face. He turned toward her tentative touch, fiercely pressing her hand against his mouth, kissing the soft palm. Her fingertips danced over the flexing muscles of his jaw, the light sanding of his afternoon beard. He took her hand, then caught the other, holding them tight in both of his as he buried his face against her palms, murmuring her name in a way that was entirely unfamiliar to her.

"Jed…" She slid her arms around his shoulders, clasping her hands at his nape, tugging him closer. Her lips were eager for his.

"Looking at your hands makes me crazy," he whispered.

"*My* hands—!" she said. His were inspired. They skimmed her face and arms as gently as the mist; they grasped her waist with the firm assurance of a man who knew what he was doing.

His voice seethed with need. "I want to feel them everywhere."

Shutting her eyes, she touched her forehead to his. Their breaths intermingled. They were close, enclosed, a world unto themselves. "I recognize the impulse," she whispered.

"The impulse," Jed repeated. He swallowed audibly. "Impulsive." He swallowed again. "Without thought."

Gussy's desire was on tenterhooks. "What?"

"Give me a minute," he said. "I know I can eventually make myself let you go."

"But—"

Abruptly he removed himself, knocking away her hands with the motion. Cool ocean air swirled around her body, stealing its delicious warmth. Her mouth opened. "But—"

Jed's expression was impassive. "You're about to become engaged, remember? This is no time to be impulsive, even if you haven't settled on the appropriate groom."

She drooped, hoist limply on her own petard. "R-right."

He looked out to sea. The boats were specks in the distance, strung like pearls on the blue satin swells. "I don't belong in the race."

Gussy held herself in her own arms since Jed's would

not be forthcoming, at such a loss she could only nod in wretched silence. She'd already come to the same conclusion—before her treacherous body had made her forget everything but physical hunger. That was all it was...she hoped.

Never mind that he hadn't even kissed her on the lips.

GUSSY COULDN'T HELP herself. All the previous week she'd been peering out of windows, spying on Jed as he worked in the garden, mooning over him, really, and even now that he'd flat out said he wouldn't compete for her attention, she still couldn't help herself.

She was dressed for the yacht club's biggest dance of the summer, in a flirty, froufrou getup of royal blue chiffon. It was a simple yet extravagant dress, sleeveless, with a low, scooped neck and a just-past-fingertip-length skirt that flared out from the narrow waist like a tutu in gathered layers of crisp tulle and taffeta overlaid with the filmy chiffon. There was even a narrow velvet ribbon in her hair and matching high heeled shoes on her feet. She felt like a Barbie doll who thought Ken was a bore and secretly wanted to date G. I. Joe.

She walked through the dimming early evening light with fresh-cut flowers arranged in a silver sailing cup, intending to sneak into the carriage house and cheer the place up a bit, à la Martha Stewart. Even though Jed's truck was gone, her skin prickled as she let herself in and went upstairs. "Yoo-hoo!" she warbled at the landing, just in case.

The apartment was messy, still half-unpacked. Gussy put the flowers down on the coffee table, stepped back and considered the effect, then tried them on the round pedestal table that Jed had moved beneath the dormer window that looked out on Throckmorton Cottage and the sea. Tidying automatically, she made a space at the center of a muddle of tax forms, spreadsheets and an open box of fresh business cards that had spilled across the table.

She paused in the center of the room, intending to listen for the sound of Jed's pickup but curiously drawn to the enigma of his everyday possessions. There was much to learn from them.

Like everyone else in the world, he owned several John Grisham paperbacks. But also a copy of Walt Whitman's *Leaves of Grass* and what appeared to be Hemingway's entire output. She wondered if he'd read them all. There were two years' worth of *Sports Illustrated*s stacked beside the love seat and a *Wall Street Journal*, opened to the stock index, on the dusty TV. The framed black-and-white studio photo on the bookshelf had to be his parents on their wedding day. A mounted hockey puck had come from the 1993 NHL playoffs. He'd rented *Sense and Sensibility*, very sentimental; that was surprising. And could he actually like that ratty, lurid orange-sunset-and-cactus-on-black-velvet Arizona pillow?

Why did she care? If all that she felt for him was physical attraction, if he was only a fulfillment of her fantasies, then why did looking at the dent his butt had made in the cushions of the love seat fill her with such swoony emotion? Why did seeing a spill of dirt from his gardening boots make her sigh?

Even though Gussy told herself that she was being ridiculous, she was still about to inspect the flyleaf on one of his books when she heard it.

Tap-tap-tap.

She froze. The sound came from the stairwell.

Tap-tap-tap.

She turned, gathering explanations and apologies, wondering why she felt thrilled and expectant rather than embarrassed. Perhaps the flowers were more of an overture than a housewarming? Perhaps she'd been hoping to run into Jed all along?

It was Percy who came through the doorway, grinning, tongue flopping out of the side of his mouth, nails clicking on the hardwood floor.

Gussy deflated.

She sank to her knees, the party dress puffing out around her, and wrapped her arms around the squirming golden retriever. "Oh, Percy, what am I going to do?" she said into his ruffled fur. "I'm falling in love with Jed Kelley." She sighed voluptuously, wallowing in her irresistible desires. "I just can't seem to help myself."

THE SHEEPSHEAD BAY Yacht Club was housed in a rambling old dowager of a building perched on a pile of huge gray rocks overlooking the marina. The weathered cedar shingles were either mossy or salt rimed or cracked. The ancient shutters were constantly working themselves loose; during a thunderstorm they clattered like castanets. The various levels of porches and balconies creaked in the wind, sometimes seeming to sway with the rhythm of the waves as if the entire structure might one day launch herself into the ocean and sail away.

To one side were the clay courts where semiorganized round-robin tournaments were held every other weekend, and beyond them, past the flagpole and the pocket park, was the open-air pavilion.

Built early in the century from several truckloads of massive cedar logs, the pavilion had aged well. Below a green-shingled, tentlike roof that still smelled woodsy, the wide waxed planks and sturdy pillars had mellowed to a deep honey-gold color, as rich as maple syrup. For dances, tiny twinkling outdoor lights were strung from the rafters as haphazardly as stars; in the arches above the railings paper Chinese lanterns swayed in the breeze, round and glowing as a dozen full moons.

At times, under the right circumstances, with the right hair and dress and partner, a girl dancing at the yacht-club pavilion could feel like a princess.

Gussy, bumping along with Andrews in a stiff, formal, dance-school fox-trot, wasn't expecting magic. A blister was forming on her right heel because her new shoes were too tight, and she had a terrible premonition that every time she swung her hips her slip showed.

Peter Gilmore cut in, but he wasn't Gussy's prince, either. While Peter was always agreeable, he was also well on his way to becoming a fusty old confirmed bachelor, far more interested in the mating habits of the cormorants than his own. Gussy's grandmother was bridge partners with one of Peter's old aunts—'nuff said, as far as Gussy's dance card was concerned.

Peter left her near the bandstand and wandered off, muttering about making an early night of it so he could rise with the birds in the morning. As she was accustomed to being more of a wallflower than the belle of the ball, Gussy was glad for the breather.

Only two minutes later, Billy Tuttle and someone's vaguely familiar visiting cousin approached her at the same time, jostling each other out of the way. If they'd been even remotely sincere, Gussy would've been flattered. However, she'd seen Grandmother Throckmorton consulting with Alice Tuttle earlier in the evening and knew this was just another setup.

Billy held her so tightly she could feel the flask in his breast pocket. Although he wasn't much of a dancer, he thought he was, and at least that saved her from making polite chitchat. They whirled around the crowded dance floor at double the speed of the rest of the couples. When they'd lurched to a stop in the farthest, darkest corner and Billy had pressed her so hard against a log pillar that she could feel the *emblem* on the flask in his pocket, Gussy was too out of breath to protest.

"Heigh-ho, Gus, you're gorgeous," Billy said, breathing hotly in her face. "I never noticed before."

"Gosh, thanks," she gasped.

Billy didn't pick up on her sarcasm. "Whaddya say you and me board the *Playmate?* It's nice and dark and—" he squeezed his arms around her "—*private* out on the water."

Gussy turned her face aside, trying to avoid the eighty-proof fumes. "Don't you have one of your girlfriends here this weekend?"

"The old lady won't let me have guests, and the Bobber & Buoy won't extend my credit." Billy slid a hand around to her breast and cupped it experimentally, still pressing himself against her. "You'll do."

"She'll do nothing of the kind."

Billy whipped his head around. In the darkness beyond the pavilion he could make out only a darker shadow, but the voice that had come from it was lethal enough to loosen his grip on Gussy. "Whozzat?" he slurred.

Gussy slumped against the pillar, her pulse escalating wildly. "Jed?"

It *was* Jed who stepped up to the platform, but a Jed she'd never seen before. Despite the sophistication of his tailored blue suit, he was all raw, seething male power. His face looked as if it'd been slashed from stone, hard and uncompromising, angular down to the jut of his chin. His clenched muscles pulsed with a tension so tangible the air seemed to crackle.

"I know you," Billy said, backing away from Gussy.

"You were in the solarium that day at Throckmorton Cottage. Your name's, uh—"

"Machine Gun," Gussy said. And now she knew why. On the ice, Jed must have been a barely controlled fury of motion and muscle. Gunning down his opponents, rat-a-tat-tat.

"You don't need to know my name," Jed said to Billy. He grasped the top of the cedar railing and vaulted onto the deck of the pavilion, his eyes blazing. Billy backed away another inch—or ten. "All you need to know is that I don't want to see you near Gussy ever again."

Billy turned mealymouthed. "Well, see, it really wasn't my idea in the first place...."

Gussy set her back teeth. She just knew he was going to say that their grandmothers had forced him into it.

"You're not going to be dumb enough to insist that she asked for it?" Jed's posture and tone were threatening.

Billy twitched. "No." He sidled off, keeping a cautious eye on Jed. "See ya, gorgeous," he tossed at Gussy once he was safely away in the crowd.

Jed snorted like a Spanish bull and looked at her. "That's the kind of guy you date?"

Stuck between a rock and a hard place, a weasel and a warrior, she was not willing to admit to the ignominy of her true relationship with Billy Tuttle. She shrugged. "He can be amusing."

"Especially when he has his hand down your dress."

"He didn't..." Gussy swallowed the denial. There was no purpose in nitpicking. "I could have handled the situation myself, Jed."

"Okay. Next time I'll let you." He turned to walk away. "See ya, gorgeous."

Funny how it sounded so much better coming from Jed. Gussy watched him go, crestfallen that once her prince had arrived she'd run him off. But perhaps all was not lost. She could still flirt her way back into his good graces. "Oh, Je-ed?" she called. "Jed, honey?"

He looked over his shoulder, one eyebrow cocked.

"You weren't going to leave without giving me a dance? Why, that would be too cruel."

"I hadn't noticed you lacking for partners."

So he'd been watching her. She smiled inside and pouted prettily. "But now you've probably scared them all off," she murmured. "They won't come near me. I'll be a wallflower."

Jed came back. "You've never been a wallflower in your life."

"How would you know?" *Little* did he know!

"I know your type."

"Don't be so sure," she muttered into his shoulder as he took her in his arms. The band was playing "Moon River." They danced with an easy harmony, a soothing silence building between them as their bodies grew attuned.

"Thanks," Gussy said eventually. "For getting rid of Billy. Whatever you think, I'm not used to handling that sort of thing."

"You usually keep your boyfriends under better control?"

He seemed to have a few wrong ideas about her, but she decided not to correct them. Maybe the new Gussy *was* a minx; it might even be what Jed liked about her.

The music was lovely; Jed was magnificent on his feet, athletic and graceful. Dancing with him should have been a perfect moment, a magical, princessy moment, but soon Gussy became aware of the glances, whispers and even blatant stares occurring behind her back. Many of the yacht-club members were simply wondering who the stranger was, but others—Vanessa Van Pelt, for one, dressed in acid green and dancing for a change in the arms of her husband—already knew. Word was sure to get back to Grandmother Throckmorton. And while an eminent garden designer like Jellicoe could perhaps be accepted socially, one with a fledgling operation like Jed's surely wasn't. Although that made no difference to Gussy's feelings, she knew it would make a huge difference in the uproar their liaison—if she could call it that—would cause in the Throckmorton household.

Give me this one night, she prayed. *Please let me have tonight.*

Tomorrow was soon enough to deal with the consequences.

7

Baby Steps

ANDREWS CUT IN.

Gussy closed her eyes. Tight. She did not want to give this up.

She opened them when Jed whispered in her ear. "Meet me under the flagpole," he said, easily relinquishing her. He tipped a salute to Andrews, glanced significantly at Gussy and faded away into the crowd.

Andrews's mouth made a narrow, straight line, but then, it always did. "How did *he* get invited?"

Gussy blinked at the starry lights. "What?"

"Isn't he just the gardener?"

"Does that matter?" She stiffened as Andrews put his arms around her and began to dance. Suddenly the band seemed all out of tune.

"I suppose he thinks he's a celebrity because he was once a professional athlete."

"You're jealous?" *Over me?*

"Well, Gussy, you're my—my... You're my girl." Andrews's face paled, then flushed, then clenched as he clamped down on his emotions. "You've always been my girl. I thought that was understood," he said starchily.

She was stricken. Apart from their interlude on the deck of his boat—nine years ago—she'd considered Andrews to be more of a friend than a boyfriend. They were companions, the comfortable, known-each-other-forever sort. It was only of late, at Grandmother Throckmorton's prompting, that Andrews had begun to pursue her more romantically.

"Both our families are expecting it," Andrews continued. "It's obvious we'd make a good match." He must have finally noticed the doubt in her face, because he paused uncertainly. "Don't you think so?"

"Andrews, I..." Gussy stepped out of his arms. She didn't want to hurt him, but she saw with a sudden clarity that she should never marry him, not even at the insistence of her family. "No, I do *not* think so," she whispered, and ran from the pavilion as if all the Lowells and all the Throckmortons were chasing her.

JED HAD BEEN WAITING under the flagpole for twenty minutes, squinting toward the gleaming lights and music of the pavilion, listening to the clink of the pulley against the metal pole and the *fwap-thwap* of the yacht-club flag overhead. Now and then amorous couples slipped away from the dance and found hidden spots in the pocket park and surrounding grounds, their trysting positions identified only by soft murmurs and the occasional giggle or sigh that carried on the balmy night air. Jed was beginning to feel conspicuous, even in the dark, and very alone.

Another five minutes after he'd started to consider leaving without Gussy, he finally spotted her. She was trudging toward the parking lot, limp and disheveled, holding her blue shoes in one hand.

He caught up to her. "Leaving without me?"

She flinched, but didn't glance up. "I'm sorry, Jed." Her voice was monotone. "I can't do this. I can't do what any of you expect of me, but I'm so afraid I will because I'm not strong enough to..." She stopped suddenly and grabbed at him, her fingers closing around the silky fabric of his expensive suit. "You must have your truck. Can you give me a ride home? I don't think I can get a taxi— Sheepshead Bay has only two of them. Isn't that funny? They only have..."

Jed unclenched her cold fingers from his sleeve. "Ease up, Gussy." She gave a shocked huff of laughter when he picked her up in his arms and carried her to his truck, parked at the back of the lot. Once she was safely deposited inside, he hesitated in the open passenger-side door, looking her over. The new party dress was limp and sodden and her hair hung in wet strings around a face that stared straight ahead without expression. "Gussy?" he said. Her lashes flickered. "Are you okay? Billy didn't try something with you...?"

"No."

"One of the other potential fiancés?"

She folded her arms, keeping her elbows in tight against her ribs. "Umm...no, not exactly. At least nothing I shouldn't have seen coming."

"You look—"

"I was sitting out on the rocks near the surf, okay?" Exasperation flashed across her face; he was glad she was coming back to life. "I'm sorry I forgot about you, Jed. Well, I didn't really forget, I was just not up to—I mean, I didn't feel like..."

Grim-faced, he took off his jacket, draped it over her shoulders and then shut the door. "Okay, Gussy, that's enough," he said, climbing behind the wheel. "No explanations are necessary. I'll bring you straight home."

"I'm a miserable failure," she muttered, hunching under the jacket. He almost didn't hear her over the sound of the ignition. "I can't control even my own life."

Jed drove away from the yacht club, turning the situation over in his mind. "You know what you need?"

"Bah!" Gussy bleated. "How about a backbone?"

He patted her hand. "Maybe tomorrow. Tonight you need a good hot meal."

She peered at him through her long, dangling hair. "Food?" Her tone was hopeful.

"Something to stick to your ribs."

She considered. "Not oatmeal?" She gave a short laugh. "That's what my great-grandfather always says about oatmeal."

"Not oatmeal," Jed agreed. As Sheepshead Bay hadn't yet been invaded by fast-food franchises, he drove across town to a roadside diner called Edie's Eats. When Gussy insisted she was in no shape to go inside, even though she looked better bedraggled than most of the clientele did fresh pressed, Jed left her to place a takeout order. They ate bacon cheeseburgers, home fries and strawberry milkshakes in the cab of his truck, parked beneath a blinking sign that read Good Food in foot-high pink neon.

"I shouldn't have," Gussy said, "but it *was* good food." She took a paper napkin and blotted her lips with dainty precision, then ruined the effect by licking the salt and grease off her fingertips. She made a smacking noise. "Really good."

Jed chomped another fry. "So you've recovered?"

Embarrassed, she concentrated on the bent antenna of the pinstriped, fat-tired sports car peeling out of the parking area. "I was, um, slightly out of my head."

"Maybe *slightly*," Jed said, now relaxed enough to tease her.

She rolled her eyes. "I had a crisis of confidence, okay?"

"Do you want to talk about it?"

She shook her head quickly. "No. I want to know about Arizona."

Jed paused in collecting the greasy papers and cardboard trays. "Huh?"

"They don't have hockey teams in Arizona, do they?"

"Nope."

"Your parents retired there?" she guessed.

"Ah, no, but my older sister, Laurie, lives there with her family. I have both a niece and a nephew."

"So you might have picked up a few souvenirs when you visited," she said, satisfied that she'd cleared up the mystery behind the garish pillow in his living room, although she still found his taste lacking.

Jed was not quite following her. "I guess. But the only one I can think of is...oh, yeah, the pillow. And the chenille howling-coyote tissue cover. And the macaroni cactus my nephew made in kindergarten. And the purple, fringed—"

Gussy was giggling. "Jed, you have terrible taste! But it's so refreshing to see here in staid New England."

"I'd like to take credit, or blame, but that goes to Laurie. We send each other the cheapest, ugliest Christmas presents we can find on the condition that they can't ever be gotten rid of. When we turn sixty-five, we're counting on holding the tackiest rummage sale of all time and retiring on the proceeds."

"What did you give your sister last Christmas?"

"Traveling so much with the team, I usually found something really terrible for Laurie, like the barbed wire toilet seat I bought in Calgary. But last year I was laid up with the knee injury, so I gift-wrapped my old cast. It'd been signed by all my teammates, complete with pornographic sketches and dirty limericks." He grinned. "No one can ever accuse hockey players of being refined."

Gussy almost snorted milkshake through her nostrils. "I am *never* going to exchange presents with you."

Feeling happier, she settled back against the seat as they drove toward home. Soft music played on the radio and the pickup's headlights sliced neatly through the darkness. Being with Jed tonight was as comfortable as curling up in front of a fire with Percy. Listening to the pleasant drone of him talk about his family, about how they'd moved from Montana to Massachusetts when he was eleven and he'd traded in horses for skates, she could nearly forget what she'd been running from. If only she could run away from home and stay with Jed forever....

"Here we are," he said, easing the truck along the driveway that skirted the front of Throckmorton Cottage before veering toward the parking court. The portico was brightly lit. "Can you get those shoes back on your feet or do I need to carry you door-to-door?"

"I'll manage," she said. She wedged her blistered heels back into the shoes but made no move to exit the pickup. Trying not to think about Andrews's near-proposal was like not thinking about pink elephants.

"Did you always know you wanted to play hockey?" she asked Jed abruptly. "Did you just fall into a career that suited you?"

He shifted behind the steering wheel, stretching his legs. Gussy's face was intent, touched by the glowing lights of the dash as her shoulders tilted toward him. "Well, yes, I guess I did," he said. "Sports came naturally to me, hockey most of all. I had to work at it, too, but it wasn't that much of a struggle. I was lucky that way." He looked into her huge, glistening eyes. "Is that what you meant?"

"I wish I'd had a talent, something I knew I could do well and was absolutely sure I was meant to do."

"Why?"

"Because then..." She bit her lip. "Well, because maybe then I would've had the courage of my convictions. Instead I've been drifting, waiting for everyone else to tell me what to do." She sighed. "And they've been happy to."

"It's not too late, Gussy."

"I'm almost twenty-five. Grandmother says that if I don't find a husband soon all the good ones will be gone."

Jed tapped his fingers on the wheel, working at keeping his tangled frustration at bay. Hearing her talk about snaring a husband, as if marriage was a commodity, bugged the hell out of him, but he didn't want it to. If he could only be impartial, then he'd know Julie's poison was out of his system for good.

"Is this the twentieth century or the nineteenth?" he asked sarcastically.

"Am I a woman or a mouse?" Gussy countered, more to herself than to him.

His gaze dropped to where the still slightly damp fabric of her dress clung to the curves of her breasts and the buttons of her hardened nipples. "Not much question of that from my perspective, Gussy, sweetheart."

She pressed her hand to the flushed skin above her scooped neckline, a purely feminine gesture, and shrugged deeper into his jacket. "I was speaking figuratively, of course."

He liked it when she got that uptight-village-virgin look on her face; it was so at odds with her amorous-heiress posturing. He reached out and rearranged some of the fuss and fluff of her skirt, listening for the quick intake of her breath, watching for the ripple of awareness and arousal shuddering over her skin. The look on her face also made him want to show her what's what—if only he hadn't decided that she already knew.

"Anyway..." She cleared her throat, plucking at the dress nervously. "What were we talking about?"

Jed stroked her leg, his pinkie extending beneath the netting of her skirt. "The way I see it, some people find their place easily and some have to work at it." Her skin was soft, giving off a surprising warmth beneath the fine silk of her stockings. "In the first half of my life, I had the first. Then when I came to a turning point, I made a conscious decision about how I wanted to go on, and I worked to see it through." Her skirt rustled as his fingers curved around to the smooth muscle of her inner thigh. "Maybe your problem is that you thought you had it easy, but now you're realizing that if you want a better life you're going to have to work for it."

As if she'd only now realized what he was doing, Gussy jerked upright, clamping her legs together so his hand was trapped between her thighs, though not quite under her skirt. He would have been satisfied to leave it there, but she gasped and scrabbled at the layers of her skirt, pushing his hand away. He chuckled easily and withdrew to his place, looking relaxed and unconcerned even though his bloodstream was laced with a desperate heat.

"I think I'd better go in," Gussy said, her voice shaky. She hesitated, then suddenly leaned over and gave him a quick, tiny kiss on the cheek; despite his honed reflexes, he didn't turn fast enough to take full-mouthed advantage of the overture.

She slipped from the truck, waving him off when he would have gone around to help. "Thanks for everything." Her glance fell on his hand and she started blushing again. "I mean, thanks for the ride. And the food, and the jacket. Thanks for the talk. I'll think about what you said." She slammed the door, looking stricken by her jabbering, then opened it again and stuck her head inside and handed him the jacket. "Good night," she added solemnly, and closed the door with a solid click of its latch.

Jed watched her hobble away, taking baby steps up the granite stairs and under the portico. Unexpectedly, Thwaite opened the door and ushered her inside. The last thing Jed saw as he drove away was the sour yet smug expression on the butler's bony face. Jed wondered if Thwaite was on twenty-four-hour guard duty or if he'd simply been spying from the window the entire time.

SEVERAL DAYS LATER, Gussy was the youngest member—by thirty years—at a garden-club luncheon meeting held at Throckmorton Cottage. Although several young married women belonged to the group, they'd begged off one by one, too busy with family outings, suntanning and sailing to spend the afternoon discussing whether to bank the lemonade-stand profits or to purchase flats of annuals to fill in some of the fading borders at the town park. It was a battle royal, with the staid members all for the security of a healthy savings account and the more daring ones promoting the beautification of Sheepshead Bay. While Gussy rather meekly aligned herself with the renegades, as the recording secretary she was too absorbed in taking down every word of the contretemps to actually speak up.

Marian suggested they table the discussion for the time being and adjourned the meeting. With his usual imperturbability, Thwaite arrived to announce that luncheon was served. The garden clubbers moved from the library to the oceanside terrace, where three large, round tables had been set up, pretty in pastels, with crystal and silver that sparkled in the sunshine. Everyone oohed and aahed.

Conversation moved lazily from the cunning rose centerpieces that Gussy had devised, to the perfect flakiness of the chicken *en croute* (Marian promised to convey their

compliments to the chef but declined the chance to introduce Godfrey in person). The ladies commented on the
wonderful weather and the fine wine and their assorted
gorgeous grandchildren. Gussy had to stifle a yawn.

Using her empty water goblet as an excuse, she stepped
away from her table as the arrival of the dessert cart deflected attention. She was about to duck inside the house
when Thwaite whipped out a pitcher from the bottom shelf
of the cart and refilled her goblet, standing squarely between her and the French doors. "Thanks so much,
Thwaite," she said through gritted teeth.

"My duty, Miss Augustina," he replied, his voice as
dry as his parchment skin. He exchanged an oblique nod
with her grandmother.

Sipping and strolling, Gussy casually circled the terrace
until Thwaite was occupied with dishing out lemon me-
ringue pie. No one else was looking. She slipped around
the corner, down the steps, and was soon taking a deep
breath of relief, safely enveloped by the lush, leafy haven
of the rose garden.

She tipped out the water glass over a mossy granite urn
planted with bright blue lobelia and a miniature Cinderella
white rosebush, then sat on the built-in bench beneath the
arbor of climbing roses, suitably out of sight should anyone come looking for her.

Idly she pinged one fingernail against the goblet, wondering what she was doing, hiding from the harmless ladies
of the garden club. How absolutely wimpish. How totally
Gussy Gutless.

Here it was, already two weeks since she'd made her
resolution to take charge of her life, yet so little had
changed. Unless she counted Jed, she was stuck in the
same wearisome place, doing the same monotonous things,
feeling the same suffocated way.

But how could she *not* count Jed? If he hadn't come along, she might have decided that marrying Andrews was her only choice. If Jed hadn't challenged her, she might never have wondered what else there was for her besides marriage. If he hadn't kissed her, she might have continued to believe that earthshaking passion could be a fantasy but certainly not a reality.

If not for Jed, she might never have fallen in love.

"Imagine that," Gussy said, tilting her head back and staring up at the heavily laden lattice arch. Even though she'd wanted her life to change, even though outwardly it hadn't seemed to, inside she was swirling with brand-new emotions. Inside she was practically born anew.

Jed counted. He counted for a whole lot.

The rosebushes rustled. Thinking the wind was picking up, Gussy turned her face to the arched opening, but no cooling breeze arrived. She shrugged, closing her eyes. She'd steal a few more moments of peace and quiet before returning to duty with the garden club.

The bushes were still rustling, almost crackling. Gussy frowned. If Thwaite was dogging her...

"Pssst."

Not Thwaite. Gussy set the goblet on the bench and leaned forward, peering around the opening into the nearest foliage.

"Gussy. Over here."

Jed was half-hidden behind the ivy-covered gazebo, casting wary glances toward the chattering sounds wafting from the terrace.

She waved him over. "Jed, what are you doing? You're our gardener. You don't need to skulk around in the rosebushes."

"I don't want your grandmother to catch sight of me. She'll steamroll me into giving an impromptu lecture to twenty ladies who believe that Jellicoe is a god and every word he uttered a pearl.''

Gussy understood his reluctance. ''But then why are you here?''

''I needed to see you. I've been thinking about you— all the time.''

Her spirits took wing; for decorum's sake, she tried to tether them. ''Well, that's very nice, I suppose, but I do have to get back.''

''Back to that? You're kidding.'' His forehead crinkled. ''I didn't think you were the dutiful type, but maybe I was wrong.''

''You're not!'' she blurted, decorum forgotten in her desperation to convince him she was ready and willing. ''*I'm* not!'' On impulse, she more or less threw herself at him. ''I only need a good reason to escape.''

He caught her, but held her awkwardly at arm's length. ''I wasn't suggesting a scandalous assignation under your grandmother's nose—''

Laughing, Gussy flicked back her hair. ''Why not?''

Jed's hands skimmed down her arms to find her hips. She moved them sinuously, trying to step closer. ''Why?'' he asked, although in truth he no longer wanted to hold off the amorous heiress.

She put her hands on either side of his jaw and tilted his head down to hers. '''Ours is not to reason why,''' she quoted with a purr, her lips parting to show the gleaming white of her teeth, the pink tip of her tongue. '''Ours is but to do or—'''

''I have to agree there,'' he murmured. ''If we don't do it, I'm pretty sure I'm going to die.''

''Well, then, Jed…'' She placed her mouth on his. ''Do it we must.''

The words vibrated on her lips and tongue and he licked

them off, opening his mouth to the escalating heat. Instantly he wanted to drink her in, wanted to drown in the flooding pleasure of kissing her, wallow in her sweet, sexy taste until he was sated. He wanted to be greedy.

Her lips moved, his tongue probed and their kiss deepened, going far beyond flirtation. Gussy must have realized that, clinging to him as she was, soft and curved and womanly, the contact igniting every nerve ending of his body. He battled his instinct to claim her.

Despite such rampaging urges, he knew he had to find the precise way to please her beyond all others. He wanted her moving under him, shivering with desires too powerful to deny. He wanted his name to be the only one that came to her lips, his face the only one she saw. He wanted to be the one man in her heart, in her mind, in her blood.

Safely sheltered by the arbor, he sank slowly onto the white wooden bench. Gussy sagged against him. "Hold on to me," she panted, brushing her fingers over his sheared hair, across his ears, down to his nape. Her long, honey-brown hair flowed around his upturned face when she bent to kiss the prickly crown of his head.

"I will." He rolled his face against her breasts, luxuriating in the yielding contours of her flesh. He covered each breast with a palm, cupping and squeezing. A response quaked deep inside of her and rose to the surface, trembling across her skin. He popped open several of the tiny buttons of her lace blouse and slid his hand back in place—inside the loosened blouse. "I'll hold you, Gussy, sweetheart," he promised, his voice thick with reckless need as his fingers tightened on her. "I'll hold you."

"Don't—*oh!*" When he rubbed his thumb against her nipple, she gasped and grabbed at the crisscrossed laths of the arbor. Pink petals drifted down on them. "Don't let go."

He wrapped one arm around her hips, taking her between his legs, her thighs pressed to the straining ache of his arousal. She whimpered at her imprudence, but nonetheless moved against him, her breasts tantalizing his lips. He took the fullness of one breast into his open mouth and laved its pink crest through the flimsy lace of her bra. Gussy arched toward him.

"My lord! Ethel, do you see...? No, no—don't look!"

Mouth pouting, eyes sultry, Gussy turned and looked into the horrified faces of two garden-club members who'd strolled into the rose garden, unaware. She stiffened, stumbled back a half step and stopped, suddenly acutely conscious that her blouse was falling off her shoulders and Jed's face was still buried at her breasts. He started to rise and she quickly pushed him back down, shoving him aside so forcefully his leg bumped the goblet she'd left on the bench. It shattered on the stones.

"Oh, please, oh, please..." Gussy turned her back on the ladies as she hastily pulled herself together. "Don't let them see you," she pleaded with Jed, not looking at him herself, either, as she buttoned and tucked haphazardly. She licked her tingling lips and turned to make craven apologies, one arm extended behind her back as she pressed on Jed's shoulder to keep him out of sight.

"My lord, Ethel, that's Marian's granddaughter!"

"April?" Ethel said, squinting myopically at the amorous young people hidden in the shadows of the rose arbor.

"Not April. Augustina, the quiet one. Why, I never!"

I never, either, Gussy thought with a dreadful sinking feeling. And once her grandmother heard about this, she'd probably never *I never* again.

8

Never Say I Never Again

THE FIRST SIGN that something terrible was afoot came when Marian Throckmorton broke the sacred order of breakfast. Gussy arrived at the terrace table on time, fully expecting the reprimands she'd avoided yesterday by retiring to her bedroom before the gossip could cycle back to her grandmother. But Grandmother Throckmorton was not in her usual place. Nor was Thwaite.

Gussy sat anyway, having nowhere else to go and knowing that Grandmother would catch up with her sooner or later. Ever since Jed had held her hand at the regatta, she'd known the guillotine would eventually fall. Unless the grapevine had experienced a major breakdown, she was doomed, so she might as well get it over with.

Godfrey came out of the house, clumping in his black leather biker boots. He'd assumed the job of cook for the duration of his stay at Throckmorton Cottage, and was wearing the double-breasted white chef's coat that Thwaite had insisted was proper. Godfrey, however, wore it with a studded leather vest and candy-striped surfer's shorts, effectively popping Thwaite's bubble of pomposity. Gussy silently cheered the unconventional butler's subversion.

He plunked a rack of toast onto the table. "Breakfast is served, mum," he growled in a mangled parody of Thwaite.

"But where's Grandmother?" Gussy asked. "And Thwaite?"

"Miz Throckmorton's in with the old geezer. The other old geezer's hovering outside the door." Godfrey scoffed. "Trying to eavesdrop, most like."

If Grandmother was in with Great-grandfather, the situation was worse than Gussy had feared. They were consulting! On her punishment!

There was an egg in an eggcup on her plate; she picked up a knife and took off its top with a ruthless skill born of desperation. Unless she found a way to speak up loud enough for them to hear, she was done for. More importantly, *Jed* was done for.

She could not let that happen.

Still automatically carrying on with breakfast, she took a slice of the brittle toast, scowling so ferociously that even Godfrey, king of scowls, noticed. "Egg okay?" he asked.

Gussy snapped the toast in half and stabbed a pointed end into the soft-boiled egg. "Fine, Godfrey. How long has Grandmother been up there?"

"Dunno."

"Long enough to have missed her first cup of coffee," Gussy calculated. One cup late and she'd be merely reprimanded. Two cups late and she'd be married off to Andrews Lowell before word could spread beyond the garden club. Jed was probably a goner in either case.

Godfrey clumped back to the kitchen without insisting she try the oatmeal. Gussy smiled bleakly. Maybe she'd ask him to buttle for her and Andrews.

Marian emerged from the house. "Augustina," she pronounced in drill-sergeant mode, with only a tight nod of greeting. She marched to her place, Thwaite on her heels. He held out the chair and had poured a cup of coffee by the time she picked up her napkin.

Gussy snapped to attention. "Good morning, Grand-mother."

"That's debatable." Marian's eyes flicked at Thwaite and he disappeared inside, silent and obsequious. Marian turned her steely gaze on Gussy. "Augustina, I'm shocked at you. What's more, I'm ashamed."

Gussy briefly looked away, summoning courage. "What did I do that was so wrong?" she asked, more plaintive than defiant. April had gotten into scrapes like this all the time and come through without a scratch. Unless you counted her divorce.

"I chose to ignore as insignificant the talk of you hold-ing hands with the gardener during the regatta. All young people must test their boundaries by commingling with outsiders. I'm certain you've realized it was inappropriate. And dear Andrews explained that you'd balked at his... overtures, shall we say, during the dance, so I can also disregard Thwaite's report of you hitching a ride home in Mr. Kelley's pickup truck."

Marian slowly stirred cream into her coffee. "However, I cannot account for your behavior at the garden-club luncheon. Allowing Ethel and Louise Fiske to catch you in a compromising position with one of your more ardent suitors was simply beyond the pale. They have the entire membership speculating on who it was."

Gussy stared, openmouthed. They didn't know? No one knew?

"I will not abide such open speculation on your scan-dalous conduct, Augustina," Marian continued. "You'd do well to remember that a proper lady's name appears in public on three occasions—birth, marriage, death."

"Times have changed, Grandmother." Was she so sure of Gussy's obedience that she couldn't imagine that Jed had been the mystery man? Gussy frowned deep in thought. That was good, but it was also bad.

"Indeed they have. But not so drastically that I can condone your amorous behavior. Truly, Gussy, I don't understand what's happened to you. You were once a delightful child, so good, quiet and obedient. I might have expected such an unseemly stunt—" Marian shuddered with distaste "—from April, but never you. You must think of your reputation, and how it reflects not only on your family but also on your future."

"I'm over the age of consent." Even if it was only because her grandmother couldn't believe that Gussy might commingle so thoroughly with Jed, she was elated that he was in the clear. She would have to do her best to see that he stayed that way. "And you did tell me to go out and find myself a husband."

Marian threw down her napkin. "Yes, Gussy. But not so—so *intimately!*"

"It's the custom, Grandmother," Gussy said gently. "Why, these days some women even live with their boyfriends before marriage."

"I'm aware of that, thank you." Marian's lips made a thin, uncompromising line. "Never would a Throckmorton stoop so low. I'm warning you, Augustina."

"I was only saying, Grandmother."

"Nevertheless." Marian selected a slice of toast. "Your great-grandfather and I have discussed the situation."

Gussy's hands made fists in her lap. Here it came. The word from on high. The commandment. The law that could not be broken. She'd never be capable of disobeying a direct order from that fire-breathing dictator, Elias Quincy Throckmorton.

"He would like to speak with you."

Gussy's shoulders drooped.

"You're to report to him immediately."

Her blood ran cold.

"And you're to do exactly as he says. Do not even think otherwise, Augustina."

Gussy nodded her reluctant assent. Had it ever been any different?

ELIAS QUINCY THROCKMORTON was an uncompromising man. He'd been born in the early part of the century, and though he'd lived through enormous changes as the years and the world progressed, he hadn't moved with them. He prided himself on that fact, and that though old age had taken its toll on his body, his uncompromising character had only strengthened and hardened until it was as obdurate as Plymouth Rock.

Approaching the solid-mahogany bedroom door, Gussy imagined that Great-grandfather had always had the courage of his convictions, right from the cradle. And his ultimate conviction was that his word would remain the absolute law of Throckmorton Cottage and its inhabitants even upon his death.

Gussy feared that she would have to be the first to do what not even Grandmother or April had managed. Unless she wanted to be married to the man of Great-grandfather's choice, she would have to tell him no.

She doubted that she could do it. Yet she had to. *She absolutely had to.*

Rozalinda came out the door before Gussy got up the nerve to knock. "Is he waiting for me?" she whispered to the nurse.

For once, Rozalinda's natural cheer was subdued. "You watch yourself, Gussy. Elias be in a very bad mood."

"I was afraid he would be." Gussy felt shaky, but at least her teeth weren't chattering.

"Now, none of that. You go in there and let him have his say. Words are not'ing, they roll off you if you let them, girl."

"But I can't help taking them to heart."

"No, no." Rozalinda gave Gussy's shoulders a healthy squeeze. "Keep your heart open only to what matters. Try not to let this old man intimidate you."

This old man was going to play knickknack with her life.

"Thanks, Rozalinda. I'll do my best." Gussy firmed her resolve. "Is Nurse Schwarthoff already inside?"

"She is gettin' the breakfast tray. If you're quick, you can be in and out before she come back." Rozalinda offered one last encouraging smile before hurrying away.

Stalling, her hand on the doorknob, Gussy watched the roly-poly Jamaican nurse depart. One of Elias Throckmorton's peculiarities was that he insisted on British butlers, Finnish housekeepers, French cooks, Japanese gardeners, Italian chauffeurs, Austrian ski instructors, Swiss accountants...which had tended to turn the busiest years of Throckmorton Cottage into a microcosm of the United Nations. The only problem being that many of them kept quitting, reducing even E. Q. Throckmorton to accepting whatever nationality his money could buy. Now, Rozalinda was his favorite, if such a curmudgeon could be said to have favorites.

Gussy wondered if Jed would consider changing his name to Yashimoto if the need arose, then had to laugh at herself. This abiding fear of hers was making her brain spin in positively silly directions, and how ridiculous was that?

For all his blustering demands, Great-grandfather was a sickly old man, almost always bedridden. He couldn't put words in her mouth, he couldn't force her down the aisle,

he couldn't *really* make her do anything she didn't want
to do.

Only her own pusillanimous lack of willpower could
accomplish that.

SEVERAL HOURS LATER, Gussy was once again inspecting
Jed's apartment without his presence. *But I have a good
excuse this time,* she told herself, opening kitchen cup-
boards and finding that Jed's supplies were inadequate for
her needs. Chuckling at the Popsicle-stick cuckoo clock,
she started a list.

Gussy was stimulated by the daring of her intentions.

She'd stood quiet as a mouse at the foot of Great-
grandfather's draped Louis XV four-poster as he read her
the riot act on the proper way for an unmarried female
Throckmorton to behave. His voice had boomed inside her
head like a cannon and he'd stomped his cane on the carpet
and once even shook his fist at her. She'd trembled in her
shoes as always, but at least she'd stood her ground, even
when the ultimatum was issued. Her tongue-tied silence
was naturally taken for obedience, and indeed it may have
been. She'd been too intimidated at the time to notice the
loophole in his edict. Finally she'd skulked out of the darkened, swaddled bedroom when Great-grandfather bellowed
to Schwarthoff for his breakfast tray, dismissing Gussy
with the frown of his tangled white eyebrows.

Now, having decided once again to take her life in her
own hands, but in a way that would also technically follow
her grandparents' orders, Gussy intended to strike immediately. If she waited even one day, her bold plan could
collapse. Andrews might show up to ask for her hand in
marriage, and it was distinctly possible she wouldn't dare
turn him down.

Gussy returned to Throckmorton Cottage through the

service entrance, being careful to avoid Grandmother, who was likely at her desk in the library arranging things with her dear Andrews. That didn't give Gussy much leeway to arrange her own future.

She conferred with Godfrey, then dispatched him to the carriage house with a carton of groceries, kitchen utensils and a heavy skillet, with Percy tugging at his leash. Watching out for Thwaite, she dared a quick trip up to her bedroom to snatch her sexiest dress out of the closet, then slipped from the house unseen. If all went as planned, she'd return inviolable.

Godfrey stayed long enough to get her started, then left looking doubtful about her abilities to cook the pasta and vegetables without *over*cooking them. She waved him off, professing confidence in the skills she'd picked up from watching their various French chefs. She actually wanted Godfrey out of the way; she had no idea when Jed would return home from his consultation about a big job with the Pequot Heritage Committee. For company, she kept Percy. He calmed her.

She promised herself that Grandmother Throckmorton, having already exhibited a lack of awareness where Jed was concerned, would never think to look for Gussy here at the carriage house. How anyone—even a seventy-year-old woman—could look at Jed and not understand that he was too vital to be bound by Victorian Era class restrictions was beyond her comprehension. But perhaps she was lucky that Grandmother's imagination was so narrow; it had given Gussy her narrow window of opportunity.

Now if only Jed was as compliant...

Gussy was hoping that the way he'd kissed her in the arbor meant that he would be. In fact, she was counting on it—this whole deal was an all-or-nothing sort of gamble.

All was Jed. *Nothing* was poor Andrews. No, she thought, *nothing* was Gussy the Pusillanimouse, left with what she deserved.

Percy finished his inspection of the apartment and flopped onto an Oriental rug that was too shabby even for the big house. Gussy double-checked the progress of dinner, then went to wash and change her clothes. There was no soap, so she rummaged in the bathroom cabinets until she found a cache of tiny hotel soaps. She supposed everyone had unusual personal habits; if this was the worst of Jed's she could happily accommodate it.

In the living room, Gussy sorted through his CDs—the Weird Al Yankovic had to have come from his sister—and selected the only classical recording he owned. Then she changed her mind and tried an Irish group, the Corrs. *Better.* Their rollicking violins and traditional jigs lightened the mood. The music might even make her forget that tonight her entire future was at stake.

She returned to the kitchen to finish slicing the zucchini and yellow squash. She chopped basil. "Runaway" came on, a catchy but poignant song about a girl who'd run away from everything for the man she loved. The lyrics made Gussy forget her recipe card and begin questioning herself. If Jed complied, could she say goodbye to the comfortable life-style to which she was accustomed? Could she leave her home and family behind?

The thought gave her an edge-of-the-precipice feeling in the pit of her stomach. She wondered if she would find it easier to run away now that she knew what she was running toward.

"Yes, of course," she murmured, thinking of Jed. He was strong. His urging was the impetus she needed to break out of her pattern of inertia.

Which had been the crux of her first marriage plan.

She'd intended to rely on the bonds of matrimony to give her the courage to declare her independence. Once she had her own house and her own husband, surely her own identity would follow.

"Don't you think, Percy?" she asked, wondering if she'd missed a crucial step in her calculations of the current plan or if the worry nibbling at her confidence was only due to nerves. The dog's ears went up at the sound of an engine below.

Gussy's spine tingled. Certainly just nerves.

Jed was home.

"WELL, WHAT'S THIS?" Jed said when he came through the door. "A pleasant surprise."

"I'm glad it's that and not an unwelcome one," Gussy quickly replied, her hands clasped behind her back. She looked nervous, excited, wary, desirable—all at once. "I hope you don't mind that I let myself in."

Percy nudged his head against Jed's palm. "Not if that's dinner I smell." He sniffed, identifying olive oil and garlic. Percy was friendly and Gussy was lovely, her eyes huge and her lips soft and vulnerable. Standing barefooted in a long, slinky, sage green dress with a deep V neckline, she was more than a pleasant surprise.

"Does this mean that Ethel and Louise haven't reported in yet to your grandmother?" he asked. Gussy had been so flustered over the incident he'd figured that he wouldn't see her again for weeks. Her reaction had made him decide once and for all that she could not possibly be quite as practiced an amorous heiress as he'd first believed.

"Oh, they blabbed, all right. And fast." He followed her into the kitchen. "Everyone's talking about Gussy Fairchild's wild romantic encounter in the rose garden. But you'll be glad to know that they didn't get a clear look at you. I'm in terribly hot water with my grandparents, but at least your job is safe.''

Jed leaned against the counter and surveyed the various small heaps of vegetables and herbs. ''I wasn't particularly concerned about the job, Gussy, but is that really why you didn't want my identity revealed?'' His voice deepened a notch. ''I thought that you were worried about being caught consorting with the gardener. Seeing as how the Throckmortons are stuck in the nineteenth century...''

Her lashes fluttered as she stared into a steaming pot of pasta. ''Not at all, Jed. Or at least, not entirely. I can't help what Great-grandfather and Grandmother think. As for me...'' She glanced up, her cheeks rosy and damp, her glasses fogged. ''I—I...*admire you greatly.*''

He chuckled. The quaintness of the phrase brought to mind the older sister in *Sense and Sensibility,* a movie he'd recently rented because he'd never read Jane Austen and all the copies of the action/adventure blockbusters were gone, anyhow. Come to think of it, Gussy's personality could be likened to both of the sisters in the movie; she was sense one minute, susceptible, high-strung, quivering sensibility the next.

''I admire you greatly, too,'' he said carefully.

She fiddled with pot holders. ''That's good, then. That's settled.''

Jed levered himself away from the counter. ''I wouldn't go that far, Miss Augustina.'' He ambled into the living room. ''Nothing's settled between us. Yet.'' When he looked back into the kitchen, she was rubbing frantically at her glasses, her cheeks glowing bright pink. ''Have I got time for a shower before dinner?'' Percy tapped down the narrow hallway, his tail swishing against the walls.

''Go ahead.'' Gussy shoved her glasses crookedly back in place. ''I'm, uh, I've got everything under control.'' She smiled bravely, making shooing motions toward the bath-room. "Take your shower." She looked at him, then at his half-unbuttoned shirt, a more explicit picture clearly forming in her mind. "Oh, gosh," she said in a small voice.

Jed was grinning when he turned away. Definitely not a calculating femme fatale, but still an heiress, and as for amorous…yes, she was amorous, and maybe, just maybe, exclusively. Feeling immensely relieved, he slapped the dog's flank as they passed in the hall.

A man could do worse than come home to a friendly dog, a home-cooked meal and an amorous heiress.

THE SOAP WAS MISSING again, for the third time—all co-inciding with Gussy's visits, if he counted the day she'd dropped off the flowers. He checked the shower-stall soap dish. Also empty. This was very strange. Could Gussy have some kind of secret, kinky predilection for his used soaps?

"Ah, say, Gussy?" he called. "You seen the soap?"

The oven door creaked. "I just unwrapped a fresh one."

Obviously a lie. "No, you didn't, sweetheart," he mut-tered as he took another of the slim hotel giveaways out of the cabinet. Someday soon he'd reach the bottom of the stash, now that he was no longer traveling with the team. He wondered if Gussy had a thing for big bar soap, too. He adjusted the water temperature, shaking his head. Very, very strange.

By the time he was clean and dressed, Gussy had fin-ished the meal and set the table. She produced a pitcher of planter's punch from the fridge, and they brought tall, frosty glasses of it into the living room. He took the love seat; she hesitated, sense warring with sensibility, and sat in the armchair. Percy squatted on his haunches beside the love seat and tried to lick Jed's hands and his arms below the pushed-up sleeves of his striped jersey, making whimpering, yearning sounds in his throat when Jed said no.

"Percy, come here, baby," Gussy coaxed, patting her thigh. The dog curled up at her feet, licking his chops contentedly. She looked apologetically at Jed. "He likes the taste of skin."

Jed's glance slid along the smooth curves of her arms, her throat, her cheeks. "I've noticed."

Her ice cubes clinked; she had to put both hands on the glass to hold it steady. Silence stretched between them. "Did you have a good day?" she asked, very June Cleaver.

He told her more about the project he was planning to submit a bid on, the restoration of a small 1700s settler's homestead and kitchen garden in Pequot, fifteen miles away. She was a good listener and so he elaborated, sketching his design ideas in the air. By the time he wound down, she jumped up and said they had to eat before the pasta turned to mush.

So what was this? Jed wondered as they sat at the round table in the ivy-hung dormer. A fiancé audition? A wife audition? Women did that to him all the time—cooked him meals, tidied his house, brought over baked goods and surprised him with gifts like tea towels or canister sets they found on sale that happened to "go with" his kitchen—probably because they sensed he was susceptible.

He had this image in his mind of the perfect life after hockey. It involved a big, sloppy house and several kids and a smart, sexy, funny woman who, yeah, okay, knew how to cook, but more importantly was warm and sweet and genuine as her baked-from-scratch-with-fresh-ingredients brownies. Probably a large part of this image had to do with his parents' chaotic household, their strong relationship and their complete lack of pretension.

Julie Cole had filled the bill, at first. She was a nice, friendly, pretty girl who didn't seem overly impressed with his status as a professional athlete and was openly appreciative but not hung up on his expensive condo and new Porsche. She was a good-time gal, all right, but she'd been young, maybe naive, just feeling her oats—or so he'd thought. Only when he was out of that life for good did he come to realize that Julie didn't want him without it. He still wasn't sure if she'd been that way all along and her sweet nature was just a ruse or if she'd simply become too accustomed to the good life to give it up for a more ordinary existence in the boondocks of Maine. Maybe the whole fiasco was partly his own fault.

On the other hand, he'd been leery of Gussy from the start. He'd started out intending to steer clear of her, and look where that had landed him. But he couldn't say that he was sorry. So far, Gussy had turned more and more into the kind of woman he could fall hard and possibly painfully for, like a referee on the bottom of a pileup—unlike Julie, who'd gone in the other direction until his feelings for her were dry and flat and bitter as dirt.

"Is a meal without meat okay with you?" Gussy asked, bringing platters to the table. "I'm a sort-of vegetarian."

He took a large helping of the bow-tie-shaped pasta. "It's fine, but what's a sort-of vegetarian?"

"It means I sort of don't eat meat when it's on a plate in front of me. Grandmother thinks that vegetarianism is a fad. Great-grandfather won't even entertain the idea."

"You ate that cheeseburger the other night."

"Yes, I also sort of have no willpower when it comes to junk food." She wrinkled her nose, passing a dish of grated parmigian and romano cheeses. "In case you haven't already guessed, I can be rather wishy-washy regarding all kinds of things."

Jed sprinkled the cheese over his pasta and took a breadstick. "So if you're served meat even when you don't want it, why don't you move out to where you can set your own rules?"

She looked down, rolling her lower lip between her teeth doubtfully. "I do make plans to move, but they usually don't go beyond my head. I don't actually want to leave— I love Throckmorton Cottage." She directed her gaze at the brick house framed by the mullioned window. "I love the gardens, I love the ocean and I love the woods...."

"Sounds like it's not so much Throckmorton Cottage that you love as the grounds."

"True." She smiled wryly and told him about her favorite sunbathing spots on the seashore and her secret places in the forest. The longer she talked, the more her eyes sparkled like pennies in the sunshine. She revealed that all her frustrations and inhibitions melted away when she was outdoors, digging in the dirt or collecting pinecones, clipping roses, walking the beach.

Jed mentally added a few acres to his image of the big, sloppy house and the warm, sexy wife. "You should be living in the carriage house," he suggested. "Not me." *Or with me.*

Gussy glanced at the small, sloppy room. "I always liked it," she admitted. "But once when I brought it up, Grandmother pointed out that I have a lot more space at the big house."

"And you're always in sight, right there under her thumb."

"Yes, that, too," Gussy murmured, her lashes sweeping her cheeks. She passed a bowl of salad and steered the conversation to gardens, politics and movies in a hostessy way, keeping the talk light and nonconfrontational. By the time they finished a dessert of fresh strawberries, she'd even gotten him to admit that he'd enjoyed *Sense and Sensibility*.

"I cried buckets during the scene where Emma Thompson's character couldn't hold back her own tears," she said, returning from freshening up to join him on the love seat. "It was so cathartic."

"You know, I was thinking earlier that you remind me a little bit of both the Dashwood sisters. Mostly you're buttoned-up like the older sister—what's her name—Elinor, but then there are times I see Marianne's sensibility in you...."

"Oh, no," Gussy insisted. "I might have given you that impression, but, really, I'm strictly an Elinor. I'm as plain as pudding and as sensible as—"

"Wanna bet?"

She was suspicious. "Bet?"

He stretched his arms across the nappy velvet backrest of the love seat. "I'll bet that I can make you physically respond when I kiss you. You're all nerves and emotions, you won't be able to help yourself."

"Hmm." She narrowed her eyes. "What are the stakes?"

He leaned a little closer. "How about...another kiss? And if you still can't control your reaction, another one."

She couldn't contain her amusement. "I think you're setting me up."

"Hey, if you can't do it..." He shrugged.

She sat stiffly upright beside him, her hands folded in her lap, knees and ankles together, eyes downcast, to all intents seriously mulling over the proposal. Only her lips gave her away; they were already pouting in anticipation.

"I'll up the challenge," he offered. "I have to make you respond both physically *and* audibly."

"Ah." She allowed herself a small smile. "All right, then. But remember, you have only one kiss of, say, no more than five seconds in length to produce your results."

"Ten seconds," he bargained.

"Seven," she compromised. "Do you have a stopwatch?"

Jed grinned. "We'll have to wing it."

She squared her shoulders and lifted her chin, preparing herself to withstand his best attempts. When he inched closer, she held out her palm. "Wait a minute. What do I get if I win?"

"I don't think we have to worry about that possibility."

"Humph." She glanced around the cozy room. "How about the carriage house?"

"With me in it?" he asked innocently, removing her glasses and dropping them beside his pair on the coffee table.

"Ha! You wish!" Blinking, she tightened her fists and her lips, Elinor Dashwood to the core. "Okay. I'm ready. Go for it."

Jed held up his hand before her face and slowly turned down all but the index finger. Gussy's eyes almost crossed, staring at it. "What are you doing?"

He brushed his fingertip across her whitened knuckles. She clenched even tighter. "Seven seconds," she reminded him.

"That's for the kiss. You didn't set a time limit on the preliminaries."

"What preliminaries? You didn't mention—"

"*You* didn't mention them. Quite a loophole, I'd say."

Her eyes widened; she almost laughed. "You cheat, but okay. Just try and break me."

He put his mouth to her ear and whispered, "I don't want to break you." He blew softly at the threads and wisps of hair her ponytail hadn't contained. "I only want to make love to you."

Surprise nearly made her gasp. She managed to swallow instead, her chin trembling. "Careful," Jed said. "That was almost audible and I haven't even kissed you yet."

Gussy licked her lips, which gave him an idea. He wet the point of his finger before again lightly stroking her knuckles. With his nail grazing her skin, his fingertip barely skimming the down of her forearms, he traced slow, curving lines across her skin, then bent and let his breath puff warmly against the goose bumps he'd raised. She made a valiant effort to sit tight, but her body was softening, relaxing into a slump.

Jed went back to her knuckles and did it again, his fingertip soothing and sensual, his mouth almost touching her skin but not quite, until Gussy gave the softest of sighs and opened her hands, her fingers uncurling, her palms pink and moist. It may have been enough of a reaction for a win even without the kiss, but he wasn't ready to give up the game.

He put his face next to hers. "Now I'm going to kiss you." His voice was soft, husky; he let its resonance tease the delicate, sensitive shell of her ear. "I'm going to kiss you, Miss Augustina."

Her eyes had been wide open and staring, but now she closed them, possibly in defense, perhaps in surrender. Jed touched his fingertips to her lids and the tracery of veins beneath the thin, translucent skin. He felt the pulse of her blood, the surge of his own.

Gussy's face lifted, reaching toward his palm. He curved his hand around the smooth peachiness of her cheek, turning her face to his. "I'm going to kiss you," he said again, making her eyes flash open in alarm, then close indolently as he did kiss her, soft and slow, her lips going pliant and her mouth tasting like mint toothpaste for a moment before the slick heat rose unbearably and she tasted like Gussy, sweet Gussy, all fire and response and damn, his seven seconds were up!

He made himself stop kissing her, but he didn't stop touching her, his arms wrapped tight around her body so he felt the struggle she was making, her spine and shoulders stiffening, trying mightily to hold back the moan that lifted from her throat and pushed at lips too weak from kissing to hold it back. It was a deep, full moan, burred with pleasure and sex. Jed's hair prickled at the sound.

Gussy pressed two fingers to her lips. "Gosh. You win."

"Gosh," Jed said with a burst of laughter, and he kissed her again.

She arched like a cat and opened her mouth, tangling her tongue with his. "If you don't stop reacting, I can't stop kissing you," he warned.

"It's your voice." Her legs twined around him. "It's so low and raspy it gives me goose bumps. Look, I'm shivering."

He slumped against the cushions, pulling her weight onto his chest. "I took the blade of a hockey stick in the larynx. I can't help my voice." His hands had dropped to her bottom, clutching, squeezing, pressing her hard into his lap.

"Poor, battered, beat-up Jed." Gussy kissed and licked at the bump of his Adam's apple, her fingers pulling open his collar as her hips slowly rotated against him. Her tongue grazed his collarbone. "I'll take care of you."

"Maybe it's not a cure, but I sure like the medicine." She pushed up his sleeve and bit his biceps gently, her thumb rubbing appreciatively against the snarling-black-bear tattoo. "Whoa, Gussy," he said. "Hold on."

She yanked the barrette from her ponytail, lifting her head and shaking her long hair free so it spilled like maple syrup over her shoulders. "What?"

"I need to know. About the fiancés—"

"I was wrong, Jed. I can't marry any of them. I am absolutely, positively sure of that."

He relaxed. "Good."

"May we please go into the bedroom now?"

"Since you asked so nicely...*yes.*"

JED'S BODY WAS even better than she'd imagined. It was sleek and strong with muscle, golden-brown in the dim greenish light of the bedroom, lightly furred and very, very aroused. His skin felt here like hot satin, there like brushed velvet, sliding and flexing with muscle, taut with tendon and sinew. Gussy's heart was in her throat, racing with a pulse as rapid as the beat of a hummingbird's wings.

He was staring at her breasts, his eyes vivid with desire. She took her hands off him and slid higher up on the bed, touching herself, shielding herself. Although she was rather pleased with her breasts—they were small enough not to droop but round enough to fill out a bra—she wasn't accustomed to having a man stare at them. Or caress them, although, oh, my, that felt truly wonderful! Jed's fingertips skimmed the silken undersides and danced tauntingly across her nipples. His head lowered and his tongue flicked and his mouth took her deep, the suction strong, too strong; she felt his teeth tugging, the prickling pull coursing through her body until she had to open her mouth and cry his name, her voice thick with lust.

His hot mouth branded hers. She murmured in her throat. He parted her thighs with his knee, speaking low into her ear so the delicate shivers shook over her again like powdered sugar through a sieve. "Nothing but feeling and emotion, pure sensibility," he whispered, his fingers gently delving into the warm heart of her, teasing her, stretching her, stroking in and out, propelling her into a delirium of sensation.

Instinct took over where experience failed. Gussy's hips writhed against his hand, against his erection, tempting him until he was unable to hold back and came into her with a slow thrust, burying the hard hot length of him deep, deep, sliding out, plunging deeper, then again and again, taking her shocked senses and wringing them inside out until she was begging for it, begging for more, scraping her fingernails across his chest, her head twisting on the pillow as the roaring tide filled her ears. And finally the waves broke, crashing through her in rhythm with the surge of Jed's body and the spasms of her muscles and the scorching liquid fire of his climax until she was released—astonished, exhausted, replete.

"Gussy, sweetheart, I love you," Jed whispered into her damp neck as he collapsed beside her.

She rolled against him, floating in the warm wash of pleasure but sinking inexorably to sleep, murmuring his name into the green-gold light that filtered through the pine trees crowding the windows, trying to remember, yes, reminding herself that first thing in the morning she was going to make Jed ask her to marry him because her great-grandfather had ordered her to accept the next proposal she received, and she wanted it to come from Jed, only Jed, no one else but Jed....

9

Intimate Knowledge

GOLDEN SUNLIGHT DRIZZLED through the thick shroud of evergreens, brightening the small bedroom of the carriage house in dribs and drabs. *A beautiful morning,* Gussy thought, coming in with a breakfast tray. Nothing less would have been appropriate for this, the true first day of the rest of her life.

She looked at Jed, still asleep in bed, his bare brown limbs stretched to all four corners, his modesty—or hers—spared by the tangled length of powder blue sheet draped over his hips. His head was under one of the pillows and his chest rose and fell with the faint sound of his snoring. Gussy smiled. So. Jed snored. More of a raspy snuffle, really, but close enough to give her a cozy sense of intimate knowledge.

Intimate knowledge? Her face warmed as she carefully set the tray on the mattress and knelt beside it. All that she'd learned about Jed throughout their long, lovely night together certainly qualified better as intimate knowledge than snoring!

She lifted the pillow. "Good morning, Jed. I've brought you coffee. And breakfast. I hate to wake you so early but we really must talk before I leave."

"Leave?" He grunted and blinked and rubbed his hand across his face. "Why are you leaving?" He reached for her instead of the breakfast tray, tugging until she was sprawled sideways across his chest. "Don't leave."

She leaned her cheek against his chest. "I have to report in with Grandmother. She'll be scandalized if I don't show up for breakfast."

Jed bunched the pillow beneath his head. "Might do the old girl some good." He stroked Gussy's hair. "And you."

She pressed her lips to his shoulder. "I've already been done some good." Her tongue moved against his skin; his fingers spread through her hair. "Percy's not the only one who likes the taste of your skin," she whispered, smiling shyly, the look in her eyes caressing his rugged face.

"So stay," he urged, his early morning voice even rougher than normal. "I'll let you lick me all over."

"Jed!" Quick as a heartbeat, Gussy sat up and bopped him with a pillow. "You're not supposed to be so bold with a girl as meek and inexperienced as me. Use some restraint, will you?"

"Oh, yeah, oh, yeah," he scoffed good-naturedly. "Poor little Gussy, the amorous heiress. Put upon by hordes of admirers who upset her dainty sensibilities."

"Hordes?" What a joke. "Well, Jed," she said perkily, "I can promise you that the hordes are no longer with us. Zip, zap, presto, I've made them all disappear." She hugged the pillow to her abdomen. "You're the only one I want to keep."

Jed pushed himself up to a sitting position. "Is that so?"

She nodded, bashful again. "Uh-huh."

"Is that what you wanted to talk about?"

She brightened and handed him the cup of coffee. "I've got it all figured out. Once I'm married, my husband and I get control of my Throckmorton trust fund, so money will be no problem. I could invest a good amount of it in your business, become your partner in that way, too, if you think that's a workable idea.''

Jed blinked.

"Because some couples can't handle working together and living together.''

He stared at his coffee, then at her. Her stomach roiled like thunderclouds before a storm. *Excitement,* she thought. *Butterflies.* This was a tremendously important moment, after all.

"What are you saying?''

"I'm…'' She'd lost steam and had to struggle to continue as optimistically as before. "Okay, I suppose I should have waited for you to get around to it after a suitably lengthy courtship, but, well, the fact is I'm under the gun. Great-grandfather gave me an ultimatum. No, an order. I have to get married.''

"You have to get married.''

Jed was not responding at all the way she'd hoped. He was as still and stony as the sphinx, staring at her as if she'd just landed from Mars. She felt timidity and cowardice creeping up on her. If Jed didn't propose soon, she might have a total relapse into mousiness.

"You *have* to get married,'' he repeated, frowning. "I don't imagine he meant for you to marry me, though.''

Gussy gulped, trying to dislodge the lump in her throat. "That's just it. I know very well he and Grandmother meant Andrews, but Great-grandfather neglected to be specific, you see? He ranted and raved and then he told me that my time had run out and I must accept my next proposal of marriage. Meaning Andrews. I think Grandmother was setting it up with him—Andrews, that is. But since Great-grandfather didn't actually mention Andrews by name, I thought…'' *Please, Jed,* she begged silently. *Please, please, ask me now.*

"You thought I'd do?"

Although that was putting it rather more dispassionately than Gussy cared to after the past night, she nodded and said, "Yes, I suppose so." She cleared her throat. "You'd do very well."

"How cut-and-dried."

"But it's not!" she insisted. More than anything, she wanted him to open his arms to her, hold her close, whisper sweet words in her ear until she felt safe and secure in her scary commitment to him. While she needed the support to confront her grandparents, she needed it even more as reassurance that she hadn't dreamed their passionate union. Presently, Jed did not look romantic in the slightest.

She was too timid to try kissing him until he remembered they were lovers, so she tried another tactic. "Marriage will be beneficial to both of us. I could be your entrée into the local social scene and that would give your business a tremendous boost. As for me, well, you know how I've wanted to...make my own way. I'm certain that as a married woman I'll have the independence and separate identity I lack living at Throckmorton Cottage...." Her voice was weakening; she took a deep, shaky breath and continued. "Grandmother will have to admit that I'm an adult who can make her own decisions. I hope."

Peering through her lowered lashes, she watched as Jed sprang from bed as if the mattress burned with hot coals. He grabbed the jeans he'd dropped the evening before and jammed his legs into them, the muscles in his chest bunched tightly beneath his skin. "Sorry," he said shortly, not looking at her. His mouth twisted. "I don't like to be naked when I'm discussing business."

Gussy winced. "Business?"

"That's what it sounds like to me. An arranged marriage. A marriage of convenience."

"I didn't intend—"

"Your intentions were clear." His voice was thick and rough with a clotted mix of emotions. Anger was prominent, but so was disappointment. And inestimable regret. "You see me as a means to an end."

"Maybe it sounded...I didn't mean to—"

A brisk chop of Jed's hand cut her off. She bit her lower lip, beseeching him with her eyes, knowing that even though she'd tried to be so careful, she'd very badly botched laying the groundwork for his proposal. If only she could just come out and say that above all else she loved him. Her heart throbbed with the declaration, but still her voice remained silent.

"You're not exactly the sort of amorous heiress I thought you were, but here I am, manipulated just the same." Jed stepped over to the window and braced his arms against the frame, his back to her. His head hung low between his shoulders. "Get this straight, Gussy. I will never marry a woman who wants to acquire me for her own personal gain. I will never marry a woman who doesn't want me only for myself—who probably has no idea who I really am. I will never marry..." He turned slowly to confront her, his eyes burning brightly. "I will never marry *you*, Miss Augustina Fairchild."

Fire flared in Gussy's face, but the rest of her body felt curiously cold and numb. Somehow she managed to slide off the bed and onto her feet. She couldn't feel the floor; she couldn't feel her heart. Maybe that was fortunate. "Sorry," she croaked, resorting to the automatic response. "Excuse me. I've made a mistake. I'll be leaving now."

In three strides, Jed was in front of her, his hands locked around her upper arms, holding her up as she sagged, cowering inside, afraid to look into his eyes but knowing she had to because they were like magnets, relentlessly drawing her gaze up to the stark emotion of his expression. His face was set in harsh lines.

"Don't be sorry, Gussy," he said fiercely. "Dammit, don't give up."

Her voice wobbled. "But you hate me. You don't want me."

"*No.*" His arms went around her and she felt the shock of his hot skin burning through her crinkled cotton blouse. "I want you to fight. Go out and become the woman I *can* marry." His mouth hovered near hers as his voice softened. "The woman I want very much to marry."

Gussy shuddered. She pulled against his grip. "I can't," she said miserably. "I've tried, and I just can't."

Jed released her. "I know you can, I believe in you, but in the end it's all up to you."

She stumbled, but managed to stay upright. "I'm late." There was some cold comfort to be found in the regulation of her morning schedule; it told her what to do, where to go.

She gathered her discarded dress, her nylons, her inside-out underwear, feeling puny and humiliated under the laser of Jed's eyes. "I can't," she said again. "Sorry." And she fled into the living room, grabbing blindly for her glasses on her sweep toward the door, tears welling up in her eyes as she ran down the stairs, clutching her clothes and her spectacles and the shreds of her tattered dignity tight against her chest.

STANDING AT THE WINDOW, Jed watched her weave through the trees, running toward the haven of Throckmorton Cottage. Percy barked and bounded over to her, his tail a wagging golden semaphore. He was holding something blue in his mouth, ready to play, but she didn't stop. She slowed to a walk once she'd reached the wide lawn, and Jed could see that her shoulders were slumped. "Gussy," he murmured, already longing to call her back.

But, no, he couldn't do that. Even though now that he was thinking more clearly he realized that she had to have some genuine feeling for him. She would have selected Andrews Lowell for her ticket to independence if she'd truly wanted to take the easy route. In choosing Jed, she'd face more trouble, more confrontation, maybe more than he was worth. Unless she loved him.

His chest tightened. What *were* Gussy's feelings for him? She'd said little, but the passion of her response in bed had spoken volumes.

Even supposing that she did want to marry *him*, specifically, there were still her other stated reasons to contend with, reasons that, after knowing Julie Cole, he could never bring himself to swallow.

Jed moved away from the window, rubbing his palm across his bare chest. His response to Gussy's tentative proposal had been harsh, but it had been right. She had to find a sense of confidence and independence on her own. That was the only way they could come together as equals and build the sort of combined future he'd imagined as ideal.

Then why did he feel so bereft, almost forlorn? He shook his head and walked into the bathroom. A long hot—or cold—shower might wash away his melancholy. He swept aside the shower curtain.

The soap dish was not only empty, it was missing entirely.

GUSSY MOPED FOR TWO DAYS, sticking close to home and making up excuses to veto Grandmother's attempts to put

Andrews squarely in her path. She knew she couldn't avoid him forever, but she was hoping for enough time to dig so deep inside she'd finally find her courage.

Without telling anyone, she began to scout the Help Wanted ads. There were not many positions to be found in Sheepshead Bay—unless she wanted to scoop ice cream or sell souvenirs, and even those jobs were already filled by teenagers—so she began to make tentative personal contacts. Having decided that something in Jed's field was her only recourse even if that brought them too close for comfort, she asked Tink Padgett at the greenhouse if he was hiring. He eyed her up and down told her to come back in the spring.

Finding the process slightly easier now that she'd begun, she sucked up her courage and ventured beyond town limits, stopping in at several greenhouses and small landscaping businesses to ask for applications, beginning to think that it would serve Jed right if she wound up working for his competitors. When no positions turned up, she got desperate enough to go to Haversham & Hopewell, the only big-name garden-design firm in the immediate area. It was just her bad luck to run into Isaac Hopewell, ponytailed but balding, lithe, catty, a landscape architect she'd warily observed at various charity functions in the past. The thought of his infamously witty and spiteful tongue made her fumbling and nervous. He sneeringly skimmed her résumé—such as it was—blinked when he came to the Throckmorton name and dismissed her with the gentle suggestion that she stick to flower arranging and piddling with dinky town parks. Gussy would almost have rather been cut to ribbons by his sharp tongue.

Vowing to expunge *Throckmorton* from her résumé, she drove home and parked up at the big house to avoid proximity to Jed's place. She sat in the car, simmering with dark thoughts. Instead of cowing her, all this rejection was getting her mad, and mad was good. It pushed out the physical cravings and the sentimental simpering of her hopelessly romantic heart.

Hopeful, she amended. Her heart was relentlessly hopeful, which might have been pure, cockeyed optimism if it wasn't for the flower she found on her pillow each night. A simple daisy, a fresh rosebud, a sweet lily, a golden coreopsis. She had no idea how they got there, and of course there was no note, but her stubborn, hopeful heart believed what it wanted to believe. Gussy tried not to dwell on the possibilities during the daylight hours.

Only at night, alone in bed staring up at the chintz canopy, did she let herself think of—yearn for—Jed. She'd held on to a slender thread of hope, but with each day of utter failure she could feel it slipping through her fingers. Sometimes it was only the promise of another flower on her pillow and the knowledge that Jed believed she was capable that made her continue taking her little baby steps toward a new life.

Yet she was so afraid that she wasn't woman enough to meet his challenge. She was so afraid that she'd never feel his arms around her again.

It was Grandmother Throckmorton who gave Gussy the idea of working for Beatrice Hyde. Marian had been waxing rhapsodically over Mrs. Hyde's floribundas for as long as Gussy could remember, and when she finally thought to ask, her grandmother said yes, Mrs. Hyde was a professional, was in fact the doyenne of Maine gardeners. Her garden-design business had been the most fashionable in town—twenty-five years ago.

Gussy mulled it over for a day and then decided that she had nothing to lose. It was a long shot, but so was she.

Beatrice Hyde lived in a Tudor cottage—truly a cottage, the kind that should've had a thatched roof—deep in the countryside outside of Sheepshead Bay. There was no proper lawn, only a garden, a glorious riot of brighter-than-bright color behind a split-rail fence. The hollyhocks had grown far taller than Gussy, the climbing vines looked thicker than her wrists and twice as strong and the sunflowers were the size of dinner plates. Whatever Beatrice Hyde was, she was a gardener with a magic touch. A veritable green-thumbed wonder.

Gussy paused on the meandering stone path that led to the rough-sawn farmhouse door, suddenly feeling wobbly and insignificant among the fantastically oversize garden. Her center of gravity was spinning and her vision was off to a dizzying degree, sometimes wavering, sometimes sharper than ever. Was it the sunlight? The colors? Her glasses? She took them off and put them in her purse; the slight ache that had been building at the front of her skull lessened immediately.

Still, it was Jed's fault, she decided. He'd swept her off her feet, then dumped her. Although she'd bolted upright, apparently she hadn't yet found her balance.

Gussy had to knock several times before she heard movement inside the cottage. The sharp, yippy bark of a small dog preceded its owner's cranky mumble.

"Not interested," Beatrice Hyde snapped, almost before she'd opened the door.

Gussy gulped. "I'm not—" The door slammed.

She wanted to hightail it out of there, but she was down to her last chance and too desperate to give up so easily. She knocked again and started talking the instant the door cracked. "I'm not a saleswoman, Mrs. Hyde. My name is Augustina Fairchild and I'm the secretary of the Sheepshead Bay Garden Club, but that's not why I'm here. I'm here to offer you the opportunity of a...well, an opportunity, anyway, to make your comeback. And you won't have to lift a finger. I'll do all the work.''

''A sales pitch if I've ever heard one,'' Mrs. Hyde sniffed, holding a white toy poodle in her arms. She was white-haired and bigger than Gussy by six inches and sixty pounds, with a dowager's hump and a rather large, hooked nose. Her manner was so imperious, however, that even in her sensible shoes and baggy tweeds she seemed handsome in a classic Roman way rather than ugly.

Mrs. Hyde peered down her imposing nose. ''Miss Fairchild, is it?'' She started to close the door again. ''I can't begin to understand what has made you assume that *I* need a comeback.''

''Of course you don't.'' *Ego,* Gussy thought frantically. *Appeal to her ego.* ''But who could refuse one last magnificent gardening triumph?'' she squeaked at the narrowing gap between the door and the frame. ''Jellicoe will be involved.''

Gussy held her breath for the ten-second silence that followed. Mrs. Hyde made a huffing noise, bent and dropped the poodle. It skittered away into the dark interior of the cottage. ''What's this, then?'' she asked, opening the door onto the flagged entry. ''It can't be much if that old fool Broadnax Jellicoe is involved.''

Gussy went inside and told Mrs. Hyde about how the Pequot Heritage Committee was taking bids on the job to redesign the garden of a settler's homestead, and that through her garden-club connections she'd learned that Jellicoe was to be on the committee that decided among the applicants. She did not tell Mrs. Hyde about Jed, or that he'd worked for Jellicoe and surely would have a leg up on the competition.

As they went to sit in the crowded living room, Mrs.

Hyde said bitterly, "You are aware, are you not, Miss Fairchild, of Broad's opinion of lady gardeners?"

Gussy murmured that yes, she was.

Mrs. Hyde lifted the poodle into her lap. "I should like to show up that insufferable man for the nincompoop he is, but I'm afraid it would be a waste of time."

"Jellicoe has only one vote."

Mrs. Hyde sneered. "Do you really believe that the others will oppose his choice once he's made it known?"

Flailing at her last thread of hope, Gussy said staunchly, "We must try."

Mrs. Hyde's thick, near-black brows lifted. "You have spirit, misplaced though it may be." Despite the dour tone, her dark eyes gleamed with interest. Or perhaps it was malice. "What did you have in mind, Miss Fairchild?"

"YOU STOLE MY SOAP," said a gruff voice in Gussy's ear.

She jumped. Her feet actually left the ground. She whirled when she landed, gravel spitting from beneath her heels, elbows akimbo and coming very close to sideswiping Jed's ribs, which deserved a good jab anyway since he'd sneaked up behind her without warning. She fell back against the car door, closing it with a thunk. "What?" she squawked, then drew herself up with the Beatrice Hyde–style dignity she'd picked up after two days on the job. "Pardon me, what did you say?"

"You stole my soap. At least it was missing after we...the other night. And again today." Jed smiled tensely. "You were in the carriage house today, weren't you?"

Guilty. Caught red-handed. "I only...Godfrey was after me about the kitchen supplies I left there. He needs them for some la-di-da dinner of Grandmother's, so I did, yes, I went into your apartment this morning. I made certain you were gone, and I was in and out in ten seconds. I didn't touch anything—'' though how she'd wanted to! ''—and I absolutely didn't *steal* anything.'' Remembering her dignity, she finished with her nose in the air. ''Least of all your soap.''

''Well, it's gone.''

''I wouldn't wonder, with those teeny-tiny, cheapo, hotel soaps you use. It probably slipped down the drain.'' Even though her scalp was tingling and her mouth was wet with desire and her knees were melting like butter left in the sun, Gussy filled her arms with the gardening tomes Mrs. Hyde had told her to read, added the snapdragons and gladiolus she'd just cut from the garden and marched to the service entrance as if she hadn't made love to Jed only eight days and nineteen hours ago. Give or take thirty-some minutes.

Jed grabbed half the stack and stayed inches behind her, as though she'd bang the door in his face otherwise. Although it was true Gussy liked his broken and mended and broken and badly mended nose, enough cartilage damage was enough. She wasn't *that* upset with him. Besides, they were now colleagues, of a sort, and she was big enough to extend him professional courtesy.

When she wondered what he'd think of her new job— if she ever got up the nerve to tell him—her roller-coaster response went far beyond professional courtesy. It was a lot like the strange perceptions she'd been experiencing off and on for days now, symptoms that subsided when she removed her eyeglasses but which she'd come to believe were the direct result of lovesickness. If so, she was wretched with it, and professional courtesy could take a flying leap!

Whereas Jed looked hale and hearty, except for the lines of tension bracketing his mouth. The scar stood out in his tanned face—a thin white line with its tail kinked by the early crow's-feet of the outdoor worker. Stepping through the passageway that led to the kitchen area, Gussy contemplated whether or not she'd develop crow's-feet now that she more or less had an outdoor job, too. She wouldn't mind. Maybe they'd give her character.

Jed wasn't talking, which was disconcerting. She dumped her borrowed books on a console table, carefully keeping her gaze averted. He followed suit, staring at her with those electric blue eyes of his until she felt charged with enough voltage to zap the Frankenstein monster to life singlehandedly.

Standing tongue-tied beside the table, she clutched the flowers to her abdomen, fighting the softening of her heart out of fear that she wasn't ready, that he'd reject her again. Finally Jed glanced away—she still wasn't looking at him, but she could tell because the heat lessened—and picked up the top book. *"Culpepper's Complete Herbal,"* he read off the spine. He looked at the next book. *"The Kitchen Gardener's Instructor for the Medieval Household.* Whew. Got a little home-garden project going?"

Was he being condescending? Gussy's fingers clenched, snapping one of the flower stems. He certainly was.

"I'll have you know I'm a professional now," she announced frostily, and turned on her heel because she didn't dare wait for his response. She wanted his approval so badly she might as well have sat on her haunches like Percy and begged for it with her tongue hanging out.

"Gussy?" he said behind her. "Hold on."

She banged through the swinging doors and into the larder. "Have to put these in water," she said, thrusting the glads and snaps into a deep stone sink and twisting the taps full bore.

Jed rescued the flowers from the blast of water and

placed them carefully one by one into the half-filled sink. Watching his hands at work made her brain fog. She couldn't remember what she'd been mad at, why she was afraid. She could only remember the night when his hands had ignited and then soothed her fiery flesh with the same tender care he was now showing her flowers. It was too much for a suddenly amorous heiress to bear.

"Gussy?" he said again. "Are you going to tell me about it?"

She lifted her gaze to the fully stocked shelves above the sink and took a steadying breath. "I have a job." There was no reason to admit that she wouldn't actually be paid until the new nineties version of Beatrice Hyde Garden Designs landed its first client.

"That's...great." Jed's voice had cracked, but it sounded sincere. "Congratulations."

"You might want to put a hold on that, since we're going to be competitors."

He dropped the last stem with a small splash. "We are?"

Gussy sneaked a peek at him. He appeared surprised, but not incredulous. "I'm Beatrice Hyde's new assistant," she explained. "We're going after the Pequot job."

"Beatrice Hyde?" He scratched his head. "I thought she retired."

"Not quite."

"Huh," he grunted.

"You're mad?"

"'Course not. I hope you do well." He crossed his arms and leaned against the counter. "Let the best design win."

Gussy felt slightly dissatisfied, but at least they'd begun to bridge the gap between them. Maybe the distance she'd had to travel wasn't as great as she'd supposed and she *was* ready to meet him as an equal. ''Um,'' she murmured, ''so, umm, are we...?''

''Are we...?'' he repeated, his voice so low and teasing she grew bolder.

''Are we friends again?''

He shook his head. ''Unh-unh.''

No? Why, she'd show—

''We're lovers,'' Jed said, reaching for her. She took a step back, but he caught her with his finger under her chin and made her look up into his face. His expression was devout, intent only on her. ''We're *still* lovers,'' he added. ''We never stopped.''

She blinked back the wetness that had sprung to her eyes. ''Couldn't tell by me.''

''So we had a minor interruption.'' His other hand curved around her hip, down low, drawing her toward him. ''We'll make up for that.''

''I want to,'' she whispered, breathing hard. The scent of his clean, sun-warmed masculinity sank into her pores. ''But...''

His hands were now caressing their way up her back, kneading her neck, combing through her hair. ''I'm sorry if I was too hard on you.''

''No, I think I was the one in the wrong. I hurt you by my stupid assumption that you'd be interested in marrying me for the wrong reasons—''

''Oh, I'm interested,'' Jed murmured. ''For all the right reasons.'' His lips were so close to hers, she had only to tilt her face up a fraction and they'd be kissing, kissing the way she'd dreamed of so feverishly over and over again for the past eight days and nineteen hours....

But someone was coming down the passageway toward

either the larder or the kitchen, footsteps clumping like Jack and the Beanstalk's giant.

Gussy and Jed groaned in unison. "Godfrey."

10

A Merry Chase

"COME ON," Jed said, grabbing her hand and heading for the kitchen proper, where dinner sputtered and spattered in the oven.

"But that's where Godfrey's going," Gussy whispered. They retraced their steps, clearing the swinging doors a moment before the butler pushed them outward. She hustled Jed past an adjacent door and into a space so small it had to be a closet. The swinging door banged against the closet door before she could catch the knob, knocking it shut and plunging them into total darkness.

Jed felt for the walls and found Gussy's hand instead. She brought his palm up to her mouth to muffle her voice. "Don't move," she said, her lips grazing his skin. "This is the china closet."

He thought of asking why they were hiding, but decided it was more fun not to because this newly employed but still sweetly earnest version of Gussy Fairchild was turning him on. As his eyes adjusted, he could make out the dull gleam of rack after rack of porcelain and glass dinnerware surrounding them on three sides. Not an ideal spot for a rambunctious let's-make-up rendezvous.

"Kiss me," Gussy whispered as Godfrey clumped back and forth in the passageway. "But don't break anything."

"What's breakable?" Jed's homing instinct kicked in;

he unerringly pressed his palm against the soft round globe of one of her breasts. "Not this."

He could hear Gussy breathing. And when he squeezed, *not* breathing. "No," she panted. "That's not breakable."

He put his face near hers and traced her lips with his tongue. "This?"

"Oh, my gosh," she said. "Please kiss me."

Jed was about to when he heard a feminine voice join Godfrey's rumble. The interlopers weren't standing directly outside the china closet, but they weren't far away, either. "I'll set the table," said the woman, coming even closer.

Gussy clutched at his arms. "What do we do now? That's Helmi, the housekeeper. If she catches us, she'll tell Grandmother for sure."

He chuckled. "I could break a plate and you could pretend you're punishing me."

Apparently Gussy failed to see the humor. She listened at the door for a few seconds, waiting for the voices to recede. "Here goes nothing," she said, her voice sliding up to a high-pitched squeak as she flung open the closet door and darted into the passageway, aiming for the dining room. Realizing that Godfrey's grumbling voice was occupying the housekeeper in the larder, she risked a change of direction, racing down the wide front hall toward the drawing room, her thighs pumping and her behind bouncing. Jed just had to follow.

"No one ever comes into the drawing room," she promised, closing the French doors. He backed her into them, his hands spanning her waist. "Except Thwaite."

Jed lifted her hair and kissed her nape. "Don't make me Thwaite any longer."

Gussy laughed, then slapped her hand across her mouth in horror when the latch on the solarium doors rattled. Her eyes bulged as the butler's gaunt shape was silhouetted against the lace panels of the opening door. "I don't believe it...."

Jed dragged her back out to the front hall. He was thinking carriage house, but she turned up the stairway. When they reached the second-floor landing, she pointed down a long, paneled hall. "There's Great-grandfather's door. There's mine."

He visually measured the distance. "Can we make it?"

She did an impatient, ants-in-her-pants shimmy. "We have to."

They'd taken three cautious steps when the first door opened. Gussy flung up her hands, gasped, "Schwarthoff!" and ran pell-mell toward her bedroom, her skirt wrapping around her flashing legs.

Laughing, they burst into her bedroom and together slammed the door, pushing it harder than they had to, pounding it with their fists and finally turning the doorknob lock with a satisfying click. Jed double-checked it. Gussy triple-checked.

They turned to each other. "Whew, we made it," she said.

His blood was still hot. "Not yet." He glanced significantly at the massive canopy bed. "But we soon will."

"Here? Beneath Great-grandfather's very own roof?"

Jed could tell she liked the idea. "He doesn't have to know, does he?"

"Only if I want to get kicked out of Throckmorton Cottage for good."

"There's an idea. I might be very noisy."

Gussy took his hand. "Seriously, now...don't. Promise me you'll be quiet as a mouse."

He backed her up against this door with better luck. "I can't control myself around you," he said into the silken sweep of her hair. "I'm not promising anything but that I'm going to make you bite your tongue."

Her face was burrowed against his broad chest. "What?" she asked, muffled by his denim shirt.

She tried to wriggle away but his hands were in her hair, holding her still as he brought his mouth down on hers and kissed her so thoroughly she forgot her question in the dizzying rush of sensation. "To keep yourself from screaming," he said when his breath ran out, and then he was kissing her again, his mouth hot and agile on her face, her cheeks. He licked her eyelids, running the tip of his tongue along her nose, holding her jaw with his gentle fingers, pushing his thigh hard between her legs so she was pinned in place and writhed against him as his wild, wanton kisses drove any thought of propriety out of her head.

She clawed at his shirt, tearing it off him in her need to have his skin moving against hers in the slow, sensuous glide and prickly friction and deep, driving thrusts she craved. The heels of her palms ground against his brown nipples and he groaned. Her fingertips brushed through the patch of dark hair furring his chest and down to the hard abdominal ridges, which clutched and shuddered at her touch. She fumbled at the taut fly of his jeans, the flat of her other hand slipping beneath the waistband, and suddenly the zipper came open and his penis sprang naked and hot and rigid into her hands, more, far more, than she'd expected.

"You oughta warn a girl." She held him tight in her sliding fist and her cupped palm; his eyes closed and his head twisted, falling back to expose the strong column of his throat and the Adam's apple working up and down as he struggled to maintain control. "When you're naked beneath your jeans,'' she finished, her teeth grazing the hard bead of his nipple.

His head snapped forward. He braced his hands against the door, pressing her flat between him and it until all she felt was heat and muscle and straining flesh. And her own desire, coming in great, warm waves until she was swimming with an urgent need to feel him inside her.

''Jed.'' She ran her fingers up the sides of his ribs. ''Take me to bed.''

''Not yet.'' He reached under her dress and peeled off her plain white cotton panties before she had a chance to regret not wearing fancy silk or satin underwear.

They slid down her legs. ''My, that was deft,'' she breathed, stepping out of them, the motion making her derriere flex beneath his palms. His eyes sparked as he swung her around toward the bed, kissing her again like a starving man, making her laugh, driving her wild.

He dropped her on the bed and stood for a moment at the foot, his head brushing the canopy while he looked down at her. He showed his teeth in a wolfish smile. ''Open your dress.''

Gussy lay on her back, watching him watch her as she slowly untied the narrow ribbons that were threaded crosswise through the bodice of her sundress. She loosened the lacings, thinking that seeing such a virile man standing three-fourths naked among the ultrafeminine ruffles of her Sister Parish chintz should have been almost comical, but it wasn't. It was erotic.

Fantasy couldn't hold a candle to reality.

''You're way too slow,'' Jed complained, and then he was on top of her, using his teeth on the ribbons because his hands were inside her dress, scooping her bare breasts to his mouth without hesitation, although he did pause to say, ''You oughta warn a guy,'' before his tongue swirled around her nipple and sucked hard at it, and then she wasn't watching anymore as he did all the things to her that she'd dreamed of and a little bit more besides.

"I AM SPINNING out of control," Gussy said into Jed's midsection, where she'd been testing the depth of his belly button with her tongue. She swung her head up, her hair brushing across his washboard stomach. "Scratch that. I've already spun. You're one heck of an outside force, Jed Kelley. My inertia is broken for good."

"Right," he said equably, as if she'd made sense. He snagged her leg with his hand at the back of the knee joint and started lazily pulling it toward himself until Gussy said, "Yikes," and scissored her legs across the sheets as she was dragged feetfirst toward the pillows. Jed's fingers crept skillfully along the curves of her leg and slid up between her thighs, where she was still wet and warm and supersensitive. He started to open her legs. She made a demurring noise, though why, she didn't know; it was too late for modesty. He shook his head anyway and didn't stop even when she asked him to, even when she was clutching at the bedposts and biting down on a mouthful of blanket as his fingers and his tongue stroked deep inside her until she gave up and let go and screamed and screamed and screamed.

"AND NOW I AM in serious trouble," she said ten minutes later, after Nurse Schwarthoff had knocked on the bedroom door to inquire whether Gussy was ill or merely inconsiderate to the napping needs of her great-grandfather. She eyed Jed reproachfully from her sitting position across the bed. The pink blanket that had kept her screams from echoing through the entire house was wrapped toga-style around her. "You did that on purpose."

He laughed softly and poked her with his foot. "They don't know for sure what they heard. The walls are too thick."

"Well, you'd better get out of here without anyone seeing you or else they will know. *For sure.*"

"Are you kicking me out of bed?"

Gussy crawled over and stretched out behind him, opening the blanket and pressing her body along the length of his. She wrapped her arms around him. "Grandmother is going to send Thwaite up here in about fifteen minutes to inform me that I'm late for dinner."

"Tell them you have a date, then sneak out to the carriage house with me."

She sighed longingly. "I can't. I've skipped so many meals lately that my grandmother is going to think I've developed an eating disorder."

His eyebrows rose in question. "You're *that* busy with the new job?"

"I've been avoiding Andrews. Grandmother's setting me up for a proposal, remember?"

Jed rose to his elbows and looked at her searchingly. "So you just say no. What's so hard about that?"

She frowned into the pillow, knowing she was disappointing him again. "It's not easy to disobey my great-grandfather. You've never met him. You have no idea."

"Maybe I should call on him. Ask him for your hand...."

Was he serious or was he teasing? Gussy sat up, an expression of dawning relief transforming her face even though she was unsure of Jed's intent. "Would you do that? *Could* you do that?"

He didn't answer.

She checked herself. "You're right. I have to stand up

to him for myself." Even a deep breath didn't steady her. "Somehow."

"Now that you're an independent career gal, it shouldn't be so difficult."

"An independent career gal," she repeated to herself as she scooted out of bed and reached for her dress. It was hopelessly wrinkled. She found a robe, aware of Jed's gaze following her to the closet. He deserved an independent career gal, a self-confident, in-charge equal who wanted to marry him but didn't *need* to. And even though she was trying her best, she couldn't say she felt all that different from before. While she was proud of herself for talking herself into a sort-of job with Mrs. Hyde, the position wasn't yet much to speak of. Winning the Pequot contract, however, would be an impressive accomplishment by anyone's standards.

She glanced at Jed. How would he feel if the independent career gal he hadn't wanted to hire himself snatched a prestigious job right out from under his rake?

"Jed?" He was pulling on his jeans, slipping them up over the really fine backside she'd admired right from the start, from this very room, in fact. The thought made her realize that she'd come a long way in the weeks since then. She *had* changed, though perhaps the change had been growing inside her all along and Jed was only the incentive, not the entire impetus. He'd given her the initial shove, yes, but she alone had kept up the momentum.

And she wanted to continue. "Jed? What you said before, about us being lovers...?"

He came up behind her and crisscrossed her torso with his arms, snuggling her against his bare chest. "Yes?" He nipped ticklishly at her ear.

She hunched her shoulders. "I want us to be friends, too."

"Of course," he replied, sounding distracted as he nudged her robe aside and kissed the slope of her shoulder. "That's a given."

"And will we stay friends even if I get the Pequot job?" *Not to mention staying lovers.*

He chuckled and patted her hip. "Sure."

His casual air made her remember her earlier dissatisfaction with his attitude. She shrugged his hands away, turning to face him. "You don't sound worried about the competition. I guess you think I have about a one-in-a-million chance of getting it."

He made a charming what-of-it? face. "So do I, compared to Haversham & Hopewell and some of the other firms that will try for it."

She resisted the charm. "Still."

"I'm sure you'll do your best."

There was a knock at the door. "Miss Augustina," Thwaite said in the I-will-brook-no-nonsense voice that usually made her jump. "Dinner."

"Keep your pants on, Thwaite," she snapped, narrowing her eyes at Jed as he buttoned his shirt, unconcerned.

"*Indeed,*" the butler said archly, leaving no doubt that he, at least, knew what the sounds coming from her bedroom had been caused by.

Gussy should have been mortified, and horrified that he'd tattle, but the new Gussy was one stubborn chick and she had a bone to pick with Jed. "You're not taking me seriously."

He looked up in surprise. "I take you very seriously."

"In bed, maybe, but not about my new job. You might as well have patted me on the head and said, 'Good for you, little lady. Keep yourself occupied.'"

"That's not fair. I encouraged you—"

"I want to be good at this!" she blurted, shocking herself. "I know I can be."

"Look, Gussy..." He sighed. "Don't start a fight."

She put her hands on her hips. "I want to know what you really think."

"Okay." He copied her movement, his long fingers splayed over the unbuttoned jeans clinging to his narrow hips. Gussy tried not to be distracted. "The facts are you're a neophyte and Beatrice Hyde retired ten years ago. What am I supposed to think?" His smile was coaxing. "Okay, so you're a long shot for winning this contract. At least you'll get some experience out of the attempt."

She knew that what he said was true, and he *had* been the one who'd challenged her to find a job in the first place, but still she felt unsatisfied. "I suppose you think you're a shoe-in?"

He spread his hands. "Not necessarily, but like I said, let the best design win."

"And your acquaintance with Jellicoe will have nothing to do with it," she said with a haughty sniff.

His grin was smug and complacent and utterly maddening. "I have no influence over Jellicoe's opinion. He'll do exactly as he pleases."

Gussy's competitive instincts were bubbling. She'd always been a plodder, a soldier, a drone, an average, middle-ground, *B+* type of person, but now she was fired up to try harder and do better than she ever had in her life. She shook her finger at Jed warningly. "I'll have you know that I'm going to win! I'm going to find a way!"

And Jed had the audacity to laugh.

Acting out of an unusually irrational impulse and pure spur-of-the-moment spite, with no regard for the consequences, she flung open the door and kicked his cute, grinning, barefooted butt out of her bedroom, then for good measure picked up his shoes and heaved them out the window into the peony bushes. And it felt darn good.

But what felt even better was the possibility glimmering just below her surface irritation—the chance, the very good chance—that Jed wanted to marry her, after all. Surely anyone willing to beard Great-grandfather in his den must be quite serious in his intent.

THE LATE-AUGUST SHOWDOWN for the Pequot job was approaching too rapidly as far as Gussy was concerned. Her twenty-fifth birthday was also coming up, but about that she cared little. She was spending every moment she could spare with Beatrice Hyde, traipsing around the countryside, soaking up the older woman's practical wisdom with a thirst she hadn't realized she possessed. After swearing Gussy to secrecy, Mrs. Hyde even passed on some of her secrets—such as the afternoon they were putting in a bed of early bulbs and she tossed a dead rabbit into the furrow Gussy had dug. While Gussy recoiled, Mrs. Hyde had cheerfully prodded the carcass into position with her walking stick so they could plant the bulbs on top of it, explaining how old Tink Padgett delivered the spoils in canvas sacks she stored in her garden shed. It was one secret Gussy, often sent to the shed to fetch and carry Mrs. Hyde's gardening tools, would just as soon have been spared.

They went to Pequot to view the tumbledown farm. Gussy held a heavy old umbrella over Mrs. Hyde's head for two hours as they walked the grounds in the rain, Mrs. Hyde twitching her nose like a hound, poking into tangled bushes and peering at the overgrown orchard, grumbling about the lack of authentic plantings. An idea began to form in Gussy's mind, and when she went home that night she pored over the ancient gardening tomes and began to sketch a plan for the kitchen garden and grounds of the homestead, hardly daring to hope it would meet with Mrs. Hyde's approval.

MARIAN LET GUSSY KNOW that she was peeved about her granddaughter's frequent absences. It was unseemly for Gussy to be coming home with muddy boots and grimy hands, hobbling with sore muscles, turning down every chance to associate with the nice young men she should be cultivating rather than crab apples and gillyflowers. Gussy smiled vaguely and nodded and went her own way nonetheless. Marian fumed, but decided to give the child her space for the time being. In the end, there was nothing to worry about; Elias Quincy Throckmorton had spoken. This brief freedom of Gussy's young maidenhood would end soon enough, and then Andrews Lowell and his up-standing family would be there to take over the reins, just as Marian's dear husband and stern father-in-law had done for the similarly high-spirited girl she'd once been.

THAT WEEK, Gussy's relationship with Jed ran hot and sometimes lukewarm, but never quite cold. He made it clear that he disliked being held in limbo while she worked up the guts to make her stand to her grandparents; still, she continued to waffle back and forth, unable to commit either way.

Then again, he very much liked the other side of Gussy, what she called the new Gussy. She was vibrant and gen-erous, blossoming with an all-encompassing love of life, completely irrepressible when she got to talking about her job and everything she was learning. She'd wave her arms as, with Percy at her heels, she bounced around Jed's place wearing nothing but his T-shirt, rattling on like a pair of wind-up joke dentures until he had to laugh at her giddy enthusiasm even if that made her mad. Then she would yell at him and pounce on him and he'd tumble her back into bed and they'd make up in a way that was so addictive he couldn't wait for their next tiff.

But Gussy was more and more absorbed with the hush-hush garden design that apparently involved lots of research among her coveted pile of musty old books. Sometimes she was too busy to meet him in secret at the carriage house no matter what he lured her with, and at those times he began to wonder if he shouldn't have pushed her so hard, because it seemed to him that she'd gone overboard. Yet when he broached the possibility, she assured him with a kiss that her heart wasn't set on the Pequot job alone; she'd come to realize that she wanted a little bit of everything, but a *lot* of him. And she took his hand to lead him to the bedroom, and then he stopped worrying over what would happen when the committee made its decision and Gussy lost out.

11

Right Question, Right Answer, Right Man

THE SHOWDOWN TOOK PLACE in Pequot's brick town hall, with the collectively stern-faced committee lined up on one side of a long table facing the easels and slide-show screen they'd provided and the mammoth TV and complicated VCR setup the representatives from Haversham & Hopewell had wheeled in. The field had been narrowed to four finalists. Jed had made the cut, along with the slick, ultra-professional machines of Haversham & Hopewell and an out-of-town group from Bath called Environmentalia. This was no surprise. However, the announcement that Beatrice Hyde's revitalized business was the fourth finalist certainly came as one. The general feeling was that the firm was getting by strictly on Mrs. Hyde's local reputation; the others weren't worrying overmuch about competition from that direction.

Jed's presentation was scheduled first. He'd prepared a short spiel about the historic use of landscaping, complete with slides. He showed samples of his previous work and then smoothly revealed his ideas on how to renovate the homestead grounds. His plan was plotted carefully, its sweeping vistas and major plantings dovetailing with both the existing orchard and the ongoing restoration of the ramshackle house and outbuildings. Several members of the committee asked questions that he handled easily, although he wasn't as knowledgeable about authentic seventeenth-century gardens as he might have been.

Jellicoe sat back in his chair, portentously silent, his fingers laced over the waistcoated lump of his abdomen, unmoving except for the occasional twitch of his bushy white walrus mustache and the stealthy swivel of his eyes. Jed noticed that his former boss's attention was deflected again and again toward the side of the room where the other candidates sat. It didn't seem like a particularly good sign.

"Very Broadnax Jellicoe," Gussy whispered from the last row of folding chairs when Jed had finished and gone to join the rest of the waiting finalists. "I'm sure he was impressed."

Jed glanced over his shoulder. "Thanks, I guess." Gussy was turned out in a snazzy little cocoa-colored business suit with a tight skirt, her hair in a neat French twist. She looked quite professional except for having a complexion that was as white as a loaf of Wonder Bread. He could feel waves of nervous excitement thrumming off her as they watched the slick presentations of the two bigger firms. Environmentalia focused on creating a wildlife habitat. H&H's featured an MTV-style videotape and music in stereo, but perhaps a wee lack of substance. Beatrice Hyde grunted and murmured advice in Gussy's ear.

As Isaac Hopewell was concluding what had become a nasty diatribe on the failings of various local projects, Jed remembered something and patted the inside pocket of his suit coat. He took out a pair of round, wire-rimmed glasses and turned to give them to Gussy. She stared at his offering. "Your glasses," he whispered.

"I have my glasses," she said, rummaging in her tiny needlepoint purse. "Well, I have them at home."

"You haven't been wearing them lately."

She rubbed her forehead absently. "No. They give me headaches."

Smiling, Jed extended the pair he held. "Try these."

"I've got my contacts in," she said, but took the glasses after a cautious glance at the committee members. They were shuffling papers and talking among themselves, so she held the glasses up and peered through them, squinting experimentally. "But…these are my glasses!" Mrs. Hyde poked at Gussy's foot with her walking stick, hushing her. "How did this happen?" she whispered to Jed, waggling the eyeglasses at him.

"You grabbed the wrong pair off the coffee table. I've been meaning to exchange them with you, but somehow I kept getting distracted." He grinned; she lowered her eyes modestly, although she was grinning, too. "You haven't noticed the difference in prescriptions?"

"I thought…" Biting her lip, Gussy tucked the wire spectacles away in her purse. "Never mind what I thought."

"Miss Fairchild!" Jellicoe's voice boomed her name like a foghorn. It was clearly not the first time he'd called for her.

Gussy's head jerked. "Oh, gosh," she said softly. She cleared her throat. "Pardon me, sir." She shot Jed a dirty look, as though she suspected him of purposely distracting her, and began gathering her small pile of folders, sketches and colored mechanicals. "Just a moment, Jelli—uh, Mr. Jellicoe. Sir."

"By all means, take your time, Miss Fairchild," he said with dry sarcasm. Beatrice Hyde stabbed her walking stick at the floor, her large, knobby hand clenched on its bronze cap as she fixed Jellicoe with a glare. He blinked and ran a blunt fingertip beneath the feathery ends of his mustache.

Jed sat back, surprised that Gussy was handling the presentation even though it was obvious that she'd done the donkey's share of the preparation work. As far as he knew, she had no professional experience, and most likely little stage presence.

Scratch that, he thought, watching closely as she set her first simple color-pencil garden layout on the easel and gave each member of the committee a green file folder and a bright smile. She didn't have the polish of Environmentalia or the electronics of H&H backing her up, but she did have schoolgirl enthusiasm. Although her nervousness clearly showed, so did her naive belief that neither the politics of the selection process nor the sophistication of the big firms could deter the committee from choosing the best design, which she clearly and wholeheartedly believed was hers.

She stumbled at first, searching for words and dropping one of her drawings. As she worked her way into the presentation—it involved strict adherence to the restoration of an heirloom garden, but Jed wasn't paying that much attention at the moment—she loosened up and her words began to flow with the kind of infectious spirit she'd had when she'd bopped around his bedroom talking off-the-cuff about her new job and Mrs. Hyde.

Sunlight spilled through the high, arched windows and seemed to coalesce on Gussy's form in a dazzle of brilliance. Her hips swayed with a dancer's grace as she turned to the easel, pointing, gesturing, flipping through the mechanicals. The elegant upsweep of her hair and the purity of her profile were limned by the sparkling golden light when she lifted her chin and nodded solemnly at Jellicoe. His beefy face bore a trace of a smile in response. She clasped her hands at the small of her back and leaned forward, eager to answer the committee's questions, fervid about her design, frank about what she didn't know. Jed found her to be heartbreakingly lovely.

And more. As her words had sunk into his stunned brain, he'd gradually realized that her garden design *was* the best. It wasn't so grand that it would take years to fully mature, as his own admittedly would; it wasn't as prohibitively expensive as the Haversham & Hopewell design. With her intimate knowledge of the way that small-town economics worked, she'd developed a tiered plan that could be expanded as funds were raised. She'd drawn up detailed schedules and instructions for volunteers. There were lists of the seventeenth-century culinary and medicinal plants and herbs she proposed using, all documented and footnoted.

By the tone of the committee's questions, Jed guessed that they were as impressed as he. Even Jellicoe had straightened up and opened the green folder, stroking his mustache as he asked Gussy for further specifics. Beatrice Hyde was smugly confident. The startled look on Isaac Hopewell's vulpine face was priceless.

Jed leaned forward with his elbows on his knees and watched as Gussy gathered her things, nodded at the committee and walked toward him, her expression both joyous and greatly relieved that the presentation was over. His feelings for her expanded beyond what he thought was possible. Even if she could never bring herself to stand up to her family, today he'd seen that she did have an inner core of courage. She was genuine, strong and sincere—all that he'd ever wished for.

The garden competition paled in comparison. It didn't matter to him what the committee decided, which firm succeeded or failed.

Gussy had already triumphed. And in doing so, she had won his heart—should she decide to keep it.

ONLY SUCH AN OVERWHELMING cacophony of honking could've torn Gussy away from her place beside the telephone, where she was waiting for word from the Pequot Heritage Committee. Grandmother Throckmorton looked up from her needlepoint, tugging at the threaded needle in irritation. "What in the world?"

"I'll go see." Gussy reached the front hall at the same time as Thwaite. She tipped up her chin to confront him frostily, still unsure about his discretion regarding the incident with Jed, but she'd figured out that the only thing the old butler respected was autocracy. She knew herself that it was difficult to adjust otherwise in this household, so it must be especially so for Thwaite after working for Elias Throckmorton for fifty years.

Thwaite opened the door. Gussy stepped past it and screamed.

She bounded down the steps, her arms open. "April! Tony! Mother! Father!"

With one last blast of the horn, April leaped from the rolling white convertible and threw her arms around Gussy. "Baby sister," she crowed. "You're all grown up!"

Gussy laughed. Although only seven weeks had passed since they'd all been together at April's wedding, Gussy did indeed feel that she'd grown up in that time. But she hadn't thought it showed.

"Look at *you*," she said, automatically deflecting the attention from herself. "Glamour-puss." April looked like a Hollywood starlet in a strapless pink sheath dress and sleek designer sunglasses. A long chiffon scarf was wrapped around her head and neck, the loose ends left to trail down her back. She was suntanned to a nut-brown hue that was only a few shades lighter than the color of her new husband's skin.

Tony Farentino came around the car, handsome and casual in loose tan slacks and loafers, his shirt blinding white against the dark of his skin and blue-black hair. April slipped her arm around his waist. "You remember my sister, Gussy, don't you, darling? Oh—and here's Grandmother!"

After exchanging quick hellos with Tony, Gussy turned to her parents, who were climbing out of their more conservative dark green rental car. *"Mère,"* she said, using the language she knew her petite mother, a devout Francophile, preferred. Gussy had maintained a few words of boarding-school French just for these occasions.

Nathalie Fairchild held her youngest daughter by the elbows, kissing both cheeks. "April was right, *chérie.* You're 'all grown up.'" Her laugh tinkled like wind chimes. "Philip, we've been away too long. Do look at what has happened to our little girl."

"She had to do it sometime." Gussy's tall, silver-haired father clasped her in a robust hug. "We've missed you like the dickens, Gussy, baby."

Nathalie tapped Gussy's nose. "Alas, no more *bébé.* I'm so glad I listened to Mother and picked out the appropriate birthday present for such an adult mademoiselle."

Gussy's father kissed her cheek. "And where is the lucky man—"

Nathalie hushed Philip and went to greet Marian; Gussy blinked, startled. What had Grandmother been telling them? Was she so certain that Gussy would marry at her and Great-grandfather's direction? Certain enough to announce the engagement in advance?

Suddenly April let out an undignified hoot and skipped up the steps to hug Godfrey, who'd appeared in the doorway, scowling and hulking with a red bandanna tied around his bald head, an apron over his bulging bare chest and studded leather pants. Nathalie and Philip looked taken aback for a moment, but recovered quickly and continued on inside with Tony and Marian, laughing, chattering about their most recent trip to Morocco, exotic names like Rabat and Marrakech and Casablanca spilling like gems from their treasure chest of adventure.

Gussy paused under the portico. This was normally when she started to feel overwhelmed, insignificant, left out. She still did, a little. But her new sense of confidence was swelling. She, too, had tales to tell, adventures to relate, minor and provincial though they might seem to such sophisticated world travelers.

Even better, the secret of Jed was lodged firmly in her heart. It was her own special gem, polished by love, warmly glowing with the deep ruby red of passion and the luster of rock-hard commitment. All she had to do now was to reveal it to the world.

APRIL SEQUESTERED GUSSY up in her bedroom as soon as possible. The entire family had already heard about the job with Beatrice Hyde and the Pequot gardening competition, but April knew there was more reason than that to account for this new, adult Gussy. "Give me the scoop, baby sister," she said eagerly, sitting cross-legged beneath the chintz canopy. "I want to know *everything*."

Gussy looked at April's buttercup hair and clear hazel eyes, seeing beneath the surface to the easy sense of contentment that hadn't been there before, especially during the years when April was pulling off her frantic adolescent stunts. "Tell me about your honeymoon first," Gussy coaxed. "I think marriage agrees with you?"

"This time around," April said with a smug curve of a smile. She and Tony had decided to take a leisurely month-long cruise of the Greek Islands before going on to his archaeological dig in Guatemala. "I can't begin to tell you…" Clutching her knees, she shivered deliciously, then considered Gussy's new, grown-up face. "But I don't think I have to. I believe you already know."

Gussy turned pink.

"Who is he?" April demanded. "Not that stuffy Andrews Lowell, as Grandmother insists. It can't be."

Gussy murmured negatively, her lips pressed together.

"Billy Tuttle? Peter Gilmore? Erik Huggins? Michael Stern?" April laughed and threw out names indiscriminately, making Gussy shake her head as vigorously as Percy after a swim in the ocean. "Edward Peasport III? Vito Carlucci? Tink Padgett? Godfrey?" Her eyes danced. "Omigosh—not *Thwaite?*"

"Of course not!"

"Someone new then? Someone Grandmother would consider scandalous?" April pursed her lips. "A carnival roustabout? The golf pro? The delivery boy, the gardener, Great-grandfather's masseuse?" She stopped at the suddenly stricken look on her sister's face.

Gussy clapped her hands over her eyes and fell flat on the bed. "His name is Jed Kelley. He's the new gardener."

April was silent for a moment before she touched Gussy's leg consolingly in acknowledgment of their grandparents' certain disapproval. "Wow."

"Yeah," Gussy muttered. "Wow."

"How serious is it?"

Gussy smiled to herself. "Do you remember how you told me about you and Tony, the time you invited him over for a special dinner, and had champagne, and then you…um, you know…"

"Ah, yes," April said. "The grand seduction, I called it." She also smiled to herself.

"I did the same thing with Jed. Only he ended up seducing me, I think."

"Sounds familiar," April cooed, still smiling. After a moment, she gave herself a shake and returned to the subject at hand, fluttering her lashes suggestively. "So how was he?"

Gussy's mouth opened and closed. There were no words. She waved her hands in the air, her expression beatific.

April beamed. "Do you love him? No, don't bother answering that. I can see you do."

Gussy levered herself up to her elbows. "You can?"

"A blind woman could."

"Grandmother and Great-grandfather can't."

April dismissed them with a shrug. "There's a difference. Those two are *willfully* blind. And they'll stay that way until you push their noses in the truth." She paused to consider. "*Are* you going to push their noses in it? You realize, of course, that Grandmother has told Mom and Dad that you're going to marry Andrews."

Gussy groaned and fell flat again. She pounded her fists against the mattress. "I have to tell them, but I don't know how."

"You could elope and save yourself the trauma."

"I don't want to elope. I want to stand up before everyone and say 'I love Jed Kelley and you can't stop me.'" Gussy stared at the ruffled canopy, trying to picture herself turning into a gutsy, take-charge woman. Visualization was supposed to work wonders. "I want Jed to be sure of me, and proud of me. I want to be proud of both of us, together, without apology."

April took Gussy's hands and pulled her upright. "Then your birthday dinner is the perfect time to do it. I'll be there to back you up, darling Gus. And so will Tony."

Gussy sagged. All she could visualize was herself, meekly backing down. "But you know what a mouse I can be...."

"Not anymore," April said, her hands clutching Gussy's. She gave them a shake. "Not anymore."

GUSSY WENT OUTSIDE with the centerpiece, the last touch to the elaborate table arrangement. The evening was balmy and the ocean gently rolling, the orb of the setting sun shooting rays that gilded the tops of its midnight blue swells. Pots of scented geraniums ringed the seaside terrace, showy with blossoms.

This is it, she told herself for the hundredth time that day. This was the new Gussy's defining moment—if the old Gussy dared.

It was a rare occasion, having all members of the family on hand. And for her birthday, at that. Well, she'd wanted to be the star of the show, the director of her life...*and this was it*.

Unfortunately, she was having second thoughts.

What if Great-grandfather refused to accept Jed? What if he rescinded control of Gussy's trust fund? What if her parents joined her grandmother in united disapproval?

She couldn't bring herself to care about the money, especially now that she'd found a way to earn her own living, but she did yearn for her parents' acceptance and praise. She'd always wanted it; it was the very reason she'd been so good and obedient all her life. April had gained their approval with her vivacious personality and flamboyant ways, but Gussy had believed herself too dull and quiet to attract such notice. She had to be perfectly behaved instead, never causing a worry or an upset. Even though Philip and Nathalie had always shown her love, the fact was that they were also usually halfway around the world. Last year's birthday card had come from Tibet, three weeks late but with an interesting stamp to add to her collection.

"Congratulations, Gussy."

"Jed?" She spun around, searching the terrace. He came up the steps from the direction of the rose garden, ruggedly handsome in his denim work shirt and worn jeans. Her attempt at a small chuckle of good humor caught in her throat. "Congratulations on reaching the ripe old age of twenty-five?"

"You didn't hear?" He came closer, eyes crinkling and teeth flashing in a wide smile. "You've won, Gussy. I just had word from one of the committee members. They chose Beatrice Hyde Garden Designs."

She gasped. "Nobody told me."

"Maybe they called Mrs. Hyde."

Gussy took a careful step, the sole of one of her sandals scraping on the stones. "Is this a joke? I can't quite believe it."

Jed touched the side of her face, his fingers threading through the loose brown hair caught neatly by her satin headband. His thumb flicked one of her teardrop-pearl earrings affectionately. "Believe it, sweetheart. I'd wager that you're the only one involved who's surprised you got the job."

When he kissed her cheek, her knees turned gelatinous. "What do you mean?" Her fingers clung to his denim pockets. "I have to sit."

He brought her to one of the teak patio chairs and eased her onto it, squatting beside her, his jeans stretched tight around his muscular thighs and his hand placed in her lap, his fingers twining gently with hers. Here was the biggest—the only—professional triumph of her life and all she could focus on was the puckered white seams of his jeans and the calluses on his fingertips and how his dark hair looked now that it had grown some, lying sleek and flat along his skull, shining like the pelt of a wildcat.

"What I meant was that your garden design was clearly the best. You even managed to get through to Jellicoe, no mean feat. Congratulations, Gussy. I'm proud of you."

Smiling, she closed her eyes to absorb the news. Pinwheels flared on her inner eyelids; starbursts showered inside her head. "I did it," she whispered. *It's happening,* she thought. *This really* is *it.*

"Yes, you did it. You were great. I'd say sheer genius, but I don't want to lose all my clients once word gets out about you."

Her eyes sparkled when she laughed. She'd never known such extravagant praise. "I just don't believe we got the job. And here I thought Jellicoe and Mrs. Hyde seemed so antagonistic toward each other."

"That was odd, I admit." He grinned and squeezed her hand. "I'm wondering if there's more there than meets the eye. Perhaps Jellicoe's prejudice against women springs from a specific incident with a specific lady gardener."

Gussy's brows knitted. "But I won the job fair and square?"

"No doubt about it."

"And you don't mind losing out yourself?"

He squeezed her hand again. "I'll survive the disappointment."

Marian Throckmorton bustled out of the house, dressed in tailored checkerboard Chanel and carrying several glass votive candleholders. "I thought we should have candlelight for your—" She stopped, thunderstruck. "Augustina?"

"Grandmother, I've had wonderful news!" Gussy stood, keeping hold of Jed's hand even when he would've pulled away. "I want to wait for everyone to get here before I...but wait a minute. Were there any calls for me?"

Marian hadn't moved an iota. "Thwaite answered a call. I told him I didn't want your birthday dinner disrupted with such goings-on." Her gaze searched Gussy's and Jed's expressions, then dropped again to their joined hands. "Augustina?"

"But you had no right to do that," Gussy blurted. "That was the call I was waiting for!"

"Augustina!"

Gussy froze, realizing what she'd done. Her hand quivered in Jed's.

April came outside, her fists thrust deep in the slash pockets of an emerald green silk robe. "Did one of you take my soap?" Her blond hair was knotted messily at the top of her head and her feet were bare. "I wouldn't normally mind, but it was a fresh thirty-six-dollar bar of scented Helena Von Duberstein. Tony says I can't buy it in Guatemala, so I'd really like it back if someone borrowed it." Having just noticed Jed, she propped her hands in a steeple beneath her chin and smiled bewitchingly. "Pretty please?"

He grinned. "I'm always losing track of my soap, too."

Gussy stirred at last. "Oh, April—this is Jed Kelley." She brought her hand up, remembering too late that it was knotted with Jed's. Her grandmother's eyes were starting to bulge, locked in amazement on the telling connection. "Jed, April Farentino, my sister," Gussy finished weakly. "I believe Jed suspects me of stealing his soap."

The slow hissing sound that was Grandmother's escaping breath told Gussy that she'd said the wrong thing.

"It's a strange and mysterious occurrence, this disappearing soap," Jed said, offering April an easy smile.

"Positively baffling," she agreed sunnily.

Gussy remembered something from her dog's puppy-hood, not all that long ago. "Percy." She scanned the terrace. "Percy?"

A flutter of movement came from beneath the table. Everyone but Marian, who was still wooden with shock, bent to look. Percy wagged his tail tentatively, looking up at them with round, liquid-velvet eyes. A froth of scented soap bubbles drooled from his jowls, puddling on the pink granite stones.

"Oh, Percy!" Gussy got down on her hands and knees and pulled the dog out by his collar, his toenails scraping against rock and his hind end dragging. "No, Percy, bad dog." He sat and grinned and shook his head, sending soapy flecks flying in all directions. Gussy looked at April and Jed apologetically. "I forgot. It's not the taste of skin he likes so much as it's soap. We all learned to keep our soap out of reach. Percy's nuts about soap."

"In that case, I hope he enjoyed the taste of lily of the valley." April giggled. "Thirty-six bucks' worth!"

Jed laughed. "All he got at my place were those cheap little hotel bars I picked up on the road. I guess he considered them appetizers."

"He likes hand lotion, too," Gussy said. "He always tries to lick my hands after—"

Marian interrupted. "April, go inside, please. You're not presentable." Her stare pierced Gussy. "Augustina, take your dog away and then I will see you privately in the library." Each word was precise and razor sharp.

April made a face behind her grandmother's back and tiptoed toward the French doors. "Jed, I hope you're staying for dinner. We're celebrating Gussy's birthday." She touched her hair. "In ten minutes—yikes!"

He glanced at Marian. "I don't think—"

"Yes, please join us, Jed," Gussy said quickly, not looking at her grandmother. She concentrated only on the amazing depth of his bright blue eyes. "Please."

"All right." He traced his fingertip down her arm, gave her hand one last squeeze, said, "See you then, Mrs. Throckmorton," and swiftly left the scene.

Gussy turned, wavering on her feet but determined that she wouldn't be called into the library like a naughty child. "Grandmother, I'll bring Percy away, but I don't believe we have time for a private…consultation."

Surprisingly, Marian looked at the stubborn set of her granddaughter's jaw and conceded the point without argument. "Then I will simply say this, Augustina, and I suggest you listen closely. Andrews is also invited tonight, and your great-grandfather and I are expecting to celebrate more than your birthday. Mr. Kelley is the gardener. He will have no part in this."

Gussy fought to control her reaction, but she couldn't stop the words that popped out of her mouth, which seemed to be on autopilot. "Yes, ma'am."

THE PARTY HAD an edge to it. A sharp, slicing edge, the kind that cut to the quick before a person has a chance to blink, laying bare the bone, revealing the heart of the matter for all to see.

This is it, Gussy thought again, opening Andrews's gift to find a small velvet ring box. Inside was a rather large yellow diamond, cushion cut, set in swirls of gold with many tiny diamond chips and four gaudy rubies. She snapped the box shut, one quick look enough to tell her that what had been Andrews's grandmother's style wasn't hers. And Andrews must have known it; he was looking rather peaked, and he kept glancing down the table at Jed, making tiny, nervous hitches with the corners of his lips.

Poor, well-meaning Andrews—he'd been manipulated, too.

Hoping to keep this discreet, Gussy slid the ring box across the tablecloth. "I'm sorry, Andrews," she whispered under cover of Thwaite wheeling the rolling cart across the paving stones, rattling dessert plates as he cleared the table. "I can't accept this."

Andrews seemed resigned. "I didn't think so, but your grandmother insisted."

"Augustina?" At the far end of the table Marian craned her neck. "What have you got? I'm sure our dear Andrews was most thoughtful."

"I *am* sorry," Gussy said quietly to Andrews, doing her best to pretend she hadn't heard her grandmother. "I never meant to hurt your feelings." She paused. "Why don't you ask out Sally Barnes? She's told me she thinks you're quite handsome."

"The redhead with all the freckles?" Andrews looked astonished. "But she's a local."

Gussy tilted up her chin. "So what?"

"Augustina?" Marian persisted, the level of her voice actually raised. "Show us Andrews's gift, please."

Gussy stood. "As I am not accepting it," she said deliberately, "I believe that would be inappropriate."

April arched her brows. "And, goodness, we Fairchild girls are *never* inappropriate." Tony, seated beside her, exchanged a broad wink and fed her the last bite of his birthday cake.

"I must insist," Marian said.

"Non," Nathalie said firmly. "Mother, I believe Gussy has made her choice. It is not for us to decide otherwise."

Philip frowned. "You mean she doesn't want to marry Andrews?"

"I never wanted to marry Andrews," Gussy announced,

her hands splayed on the tablecloth. Inside, she was soaring. She felt ten feet tall, inviolable, invincible. Taking charge was not so hard as she'd built it up to be; she'd simply had to open her mouth and do it. Nothing could stop her now, not even—

"*Great-grandfather!*" Gussy exclaimed.

The evening nurse, Miss Ingersdottir from Iceland, had pushed Elias Throckmorton out to the terrace in an old rattan-and-teak deck chair, as he stubbornly refused modern wheelchairs. Everyone was quiet; the only sounds to be heard were the creak of the wheels and the *shush-shush* of the ocean. Then they all burst into voice at once, with cries of "How wonderful you've joined us!" and "Dear *Grandpère!*"

Elias hushed them with a twitch of his forefinger. His cloudy black eyes searched the candlelit faces of the guests; he often didn't recognize even the members of his immediate family. His gaze stopped at Jed. "You're the fellow who wants to marry my granddaughter?"

Marian gaped. She motioned to Andrews frantically, drawing him closer, intending to present him to Elias as their chosen groom.

Jed said, "Yes."

At this declaration, Gussy caught her breath and held on tight to her hard-won conviction even as she melted into the warm wave washing over her. April took her hand; Tony left his seat to put his arm around her waist.

Gussy stared at Jed, her eyes limpid, her smile trembling.

After a brief glance at Gussy, Jed looked Elias Throckmorton square in the face. Rugs and blankets were piled so high in the deck chair that a pair of sunken, beady eyes, a prominent nose and the pale, freckled dome of a bald head were all that he could see of Gussy's formidable great-grandfather. That, and the spindly fingers hooked like talons over the green binding of an Adirondack blanket.

A twig-thin index finger pointed at Jed. "I'm here to see that you propose properly."

Jed was stunned to discover that the elderly man's hold over the household was strictly psychological. He'd been imagining Elias Throckmorton as a burly bear of a guy even in his nineties, with a voice like a growl and a biting glare that could strike fear into the heart of man, woman or child. Instead, here was this tiny, swaddled figure, with a skull as fragile as an eggshell and a voice as weak as cambric tea. At most, there was a certain severity swimming in Elias's watering eyes, a faint echo of the tyrant he might have been.

Even so, Jed angled his head compliantly. "Whatever you say, sir."

"*This* is Andrews Lowell." Marian nudged him forward. "Go on, Andrews, speak up," she hissed into his ear.

"Which one is Gussy marrying?" Philip asked his wife.

"Good question." Nathalie's sleek, brunette pageboy swung against her cheeks as she looked from one candidate to the other. "Ooh-la-la, how interesting."

"What? Who?" Elias demanded hoarsely.

"The ocean chill," Nurse Ingersdottir said. "We must go in."

"Now," Marian told Andrews.

Gussy took a deep breath. "I will not marry—"

"Yes, you will." Elias roused himself to a weak screech that sounded like a turntable needle rasping across a record. "I instructed you to marry this young man and I meant it." He scrabbled at the blankets, his vulture face looming from their depths. "He will ask and you will accept."

Gussy looked at Jed, trying to send a message.

Jed looked silently at Gussy, needing none. He'd already made up his mind.

"*Now,*" Marian said again.

Andrews opened his mouth.

Gussy closed her eyes, preparing to reject the proposal because she knew Jed needed to hear the *no* almost as much as she needed to say it.

And then it came, the question she'd been dreading: "Gussy, will you marry me?"

SEVERAL HOURS LATER, Gussy reached her bedroom, grateful for the dark haven of peace and quiet. The uproar caused by her acceptance of the proposal had whirled around her like a tornado, but she'd stood calmly at its center, certain that she had done the right and proper thing. Fortunately, Great-grandfather hadn't been quite sure what was going on, and the nurse had wheeled him away before Grandmother had gotten to him, demanding a retraction.

In any case, it was too late. Gussy was now firmly engaged, and there was no way she'd allow anyone to change that fact.

She stepped out of her sandals. Unbuttoning, she walked to the window that overlooked the front garden and raised the sash. The cool night air caressed her skin as she slipped out of her yellow silk blouse and skirt, letting them fall to the carpet. Her slip followed with a soft rustle as it slid against her bare legs.

Moonlight pooled on the plump white pillows heaped at the head of her bed, revealing the long-stemmed rose that lay across them. With a smile, Gussy went to retrieve it.

Jed hadn't missed a single night—not even this one, when he'd surely been too busy fending off the exclamations of her family to sneak up to her bedroom with a flower! She stroked its delicate red petals against her cheek.

"It was Godfrey," Jed said from the shadows.

Although she flinched, she wasn't truly surprised that he was here. "April claims that Godfrey's a Cupid in disguise. Silly me. I didn't believe her."

He rose from the slipper chair and knelt on the bed, reaching for her. "He made me bribe him to leave a flower on your pillow each night, but I knew that beneath that gruff exterior he really wanted to do it."

Gussy touched Jed's chin with the rose. She swept it down the side of his throat. He successfully slid his arm around her waist and pulled her onto the bed so they were kneeling face-to-face. "I was hoping you'd continue your striptease," he commented, fingering the lace scallops on the edges of her bra.

She shivered. "Here? Within reach of Thwaite's radar ears? Under Grandmother's discerning nose? Beneath Great-grandfather's very own roof?"

"If they catch us, I'll just have to make an honest woman of you."

"You're already committed to doing that." She laughed, hugging him tight. "Oh, Jed. I almost said no!" Crushed rose petals drifted across the bed. "I was so set on saying no to Andrews that it took me a moment to realize that it was you who proposed."

"Yeah." He made a *grrr*ing sound in her ear. "For a second there, I thought I was going to have egg on my face."

She covered his face with kisses. "Never. Never."

"Do you think we'll have to elope?"

"Well, my parents seemed pleased, and Great-grandfather never goes back on his word, so since I *did* accept your proposal at his direction..."

"We should be okay, then. I've got a feeling that even your grandmother will come around when she remembers what it's like being in love." He nudged aside Gussy's string of pearls and kissed a path across her collarbone. "It'll help that my lineage is so respectable you can trace it back to the *Mayflower*."

Gussy drew back. "Really?"

"There was a Kelley in steerage."

"Really?" She laughed. "You're teasing me."

"Didn't you wonder how I got an invitation to the yacht-club dance? See, my father is the commodore of the Marblehead, Mass., yacht club, and he called the commodore of a Bar Harbor yacht club, who knows the commodore of—"

"This changes things." Gussy made a solemn face. "I'm not sure that I want to marry someone so respectable and well connected—" She broke off with a giggle, putting her hands to his backside and squeezing lustfully. "I *liked* that you were the opposite of Andrews, so rugged and sexy and physical.... Now, well, I just don't know anymore."

"I can still take you out to the garden and roll you around in the flower beds."

"Hmm." She licked her lips. "Will you sneak into my bedroom in a sweaty T-shirt and ripped jeans?"

"I won't even take off my muddy work boots."

"Will you promise never to remove your tattoo?"

"It's permanent, sweetheart."

"And will you mind if I get one myself?"

He dipped his nose into her cleavage, sliding the tip of his tongue against the soft curve of one breast. "Right here?"

Gussy smiled gently. "I want a heart. A heart that says—"

"*No?*"

"A heart that says *Jed.*" Her eyes gleamed with love. "And it will last forever."

LOVE & LAUGH

INTO OCTOBER!

#29 ACCIDENTAL ROOMMATES
Charlotte Maclay

Tired of being a twenty-eight-year-old virgin, Hannah Jansen is the marrying kind. Holt Janson is *not.* He's determined to stay as far away from her as possible—which is difficult because they're sharing a hotel room. Still, Holt has no intention of being a *sexual plaything*...until he discovers Hannah's chosen another lover....

#30 WOOING WANDA
Gwen Pemberton

John Rockman has become a stick-in-the-mud—not the romantic, spontaneous man Wanda married. She wants to be wooed again. And after finding the contents of their home in his office, John begins to clue in. He's sure he can win her back. But wooing Wanda is no picnic; things go from the divine to the ridiculous—and seem to get stuck there!

Chuckles available now:

#27 PILLOW TALK
Kristine Rolofson

#28 THE AMOROUS HEIRESS
Carrie Alexander

LOVE & LAUGHTER™

Take 4 bestselling love stories FREE

Plus get a FREE surprise gift!

Special Limited-time Offer

Mail to Harlequin Reader Service®

3010 Walden Avenue
P.O. Box 1867
Buffalo, N.Y. 14240-1867

YES! Please send me 4 free Harlequin Love and Laughter™ novels and my free surprise gift. Then send me 4 brand-new novels every other month, which I will receive months before they appear in bookstores. Bill me at the low price of $2.90 each plus 25¢ delivery per book and applicable sales tax if any*. That's the complete price and a savings of over 10% off the cover prices—quite a bargain! I understand that accepting the books and gift places me under no obligation ever to buy any books. I can always return a shipment and cancel at any time. Even if I never buy another book from Harlequin, the 4 free books and the surprise gift are mine to keep forever.

102 BPA A7EF

Name	(PLEASE PRINT)	
Address	Apt. No.	
City	State	Zip

This offer is limited to one order per household and not valid to present Love and Laughter™ subscribers. *Terms and prices are subject to change without notice. Sales tax applicable in N.Y.

ULL-397   ©1996 Harlequin Enterprises Limited

LOVE & LAUGHTER™

MOTHER KNOWS BEST—
MAYBE!

These matchmaking moms have had
enough of their happy-to-be-single kids.
How is a respectable woman to become a
grandmother unless her offspring cooperates?
There's nothing to be done except to get
the kids down the aisle, even if they go
kicking and screaming all the way!

Plans are made, schemes hatched, plots
unraveled. Let the love and laughter begin!

Enjoy Matchmaking Moms (from hell) with:

#27 PILLOW TALK
by Kristine Rolofson

Available this September 1997
wherever Harlequin books are sold.

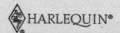

Free Gift Offer

With a Free Gift proof-of-purchase
from any Harlequin® book, you can receive
a beautiful cubic zirconia pendant.

This stunning marquise-shaped stone is a genuine cubic
zirconia—accented by an 18" gold tone necklace.
(Approximate retail value $19.95)

Send for yours today...
compliments of ⊕HARLEQUIN®

To receive your free gift, a cubic zirconia pendant, send us one original proof-of-purchase, photocopies not accepted, from the back of any Harlequin Romance®, Harlequin Presents®, Harlequin Temptation®, Harlequin Superromance®, Harlequin Intrigue®, Harlequin American Romance®, or Harlequin Historicals® title available at your favorite retail outlet, together with the Free Gift Certificate, plus a check or money order for $1.65 u.s./$2.15 can. (do not send cash) to cover postage and handling, payable to Harlequin Free Gift Offer. We will send you the specified gift. Allow 6 to 8 weeks for delivery. Offer good until December 31, 1997, or while quantities last. Offer valid in the U.S. and Canada only.

Free Gift Certificate

Name: _____

Address: _____

City: _____ State/Province: _____ Zip/Postal Code: _____

Mail this certificate, one proof-of-purchase and a check or money order for postage and handling to: HARLEQUIN FREE GIFT OFFER 1997. In the U.S.: 3010 Walden Avenue, P.O. Box 9071, Buffalo NY 14269-9057. In Canada: P.O. Box 604, Fort Erie, Ontario L2Z 5X3.

FREE GIFT OFFER   084-KEZ

ONE PROOF-OF-PURCHASE
To collect your fabulous FREE GIFT, a cubic zirconia pendant, you must include this
original proof-of-purchase for each gift with the properly completed Free Gift Certificate.

084-KEZR

LOVE & LAUGHTER LET'S CELEBRATE SWEEPSTAKES
OFFICIAL RULES—NO PURCHASE NECESSARY

To enter, complete an Official Entry Form or 3" x 5" card by hand printing the words "Love & Laughter Let's Celebrate Sweepstakes," your name and address thereon and mailing it to: in the U.S., Love & Laughter Let's Celebrate Sweepstakes, P.O. Box 9076, Buffalo, NY 14269-9076, or in Canada to, Love & Laughter Let's Celebrate Sweepstakes, P.O. Box 637, Fort Erie, Ontario L2A 5X3. Limit: one entry per envelope, one prize to an individual, family or organization. Entries must be sent via first-class mail and be received no later than 11/30/97. No liability is assumed for lost, late, misdirected or nondelivered mail.

Three (3) winners will be selected in a random drawing (to be conducted no later than 12/31/97) from among all eligible entries received by D. L. Blair, Inc., an independent judging organization whose decisions are final, to each receive a collection of 15 Love & Laughter Romantic Comedy videos (approximate retail value: $250 U.S. per collection).

Sweepstakes offer is open only to residents of the U.S. (except Puerto Rico) and Canada who are 18 years of age or older, except employees and immediate family members of Harlequin Enterprises, Ltd., their affiliates, subsidiaries, and all other agencies, entities and persons connected with the use, marketing or conduct of this sweepstakes. All applicable laws and regulations apply. Offer void wherever prohibited by law. Taxes and/or duties on prizes are the sole responsibility of the winners. Any litigation within the province of Quebec respecting the conduct and awarding of prize may be submitted to the Régie des alcools, des courses et des jeux. All prizes will be awarded; winners will be notified by mail. No substitution for prizes is permitted. Odds of winning are dependent upon the number of eligible entries received.

Any prize or prize notification returned as undeliverable may result in the awarding of that prize to an alternative winner. By acceptance of their prize, winners consent to use of their names, photographs or likenesses for purposes of advertising, trade and promotion on behalf of Harlequin Enterprises, Ltd., without further compensation unless prohibited by law. In order to win a prize, residents of Canada will be required to correctly answer a time-limited, arithmetical skill-testing question administered by mail.

For a list of winners (available after December 31, 1997), send a separate stamped, self-addressed envelope to: Love & Laughter Let's Celebrate Sweepstakes Winner, P.O. Box 4200, Blair, NE 68009-4200, U.S.A.

LLRULES

Celebrate with
LOVE & LAUGHTER™

Love to watch movies?

Enter now to win a FREE 15-copy video collection of romantic comedies in Love & Laughter's Let's Celebrate Sweepstakes.

WIN A ROMANTIC COMEDY
VIDEO COLLECTION!

To enter the Love & Laughter Let's Celebrate Sweepstakes, complete an Official Entry Form or hand print on a 3" x 5" card the words "Love & Laughter Let's Celebrate Sweepstakes," your name and address and mail to: "Love & Laughter Let's Celebrate Sweepstakes," in the U.S., 3010 Walden Avenue, P.O. Box 9076, Buffalo, N.Y. 14269-9076; in Canada, P.O. Box 637, Fort Erie, Ontario L2A 5X3. Limit: one entry per envelope, one prize to an individual family or organization. Entries must be sent via first-class mail and be received no later than November 30, 1997. See back page ad for complete sweepstakes rules.

Celebrate with Love & Laughter™!

Official Entry Form

"Please enter me in the Love & Laughter Let's Celebrate Sweepstakes"

Name: _____

Address: _____

City: _____

State/Prov.: _____ Zip/Postal Code: _____

LLENTRY

LLENTRY